THE LOGANTOWN LOOTERS

Logantown seethed with intrigue, but the law was none the wiser, and that went double for the manager of the Settlers National Bank. The venal Al Burchell and his B-Bar gang planned on emptying the vault with the aid of a few sticks of dynamite. Burchell had never heard of Morrison and Kilburn, a couple of counterfeiters who figured to empty that vault the easy way—bribe the cashier and substitute fake greenbacks for the real stuff. Into Logantown at the same time rode Larry and Stretch, the trouble-prone Lone Star Hellions. They had befriended Crazy Max, the dreamer who foretold disaster after disaster. And when the lawless went into action, so did the West's toughest trouble-shooters.

Books by Marshall Grover
in the Linford Western Library:

MARSHALL GROVER

THE LOGANTOWN LOOTERS

Larry & Stretch

Complete and Unabridged

LINFORD
Leicester

First Linford Edition
published January 1989
by arrangement with
Horwitz Grahame Pty Ltd.,
Cammeray, NSW, Australia

British Library CIP Data

Grover, Marshall
    The Logantown looters.—Large print ed.—
Linford western library
I. Title
823[F]

ISBN 0-7089-6669-1

Published by
F. A. Thorpe (Publishing) Ltd.
Anstey, Leicestershire
Set by Rowland Phototypesetting Ltd.
Bury St. Edmunds, Suffolk
Printed and bound in Great Britain by
T. J. Press (Padstow) Ltd., Padstow, Cornwall

1

AT his best, the engineer of the eastbound locomotive was a mean-tempered veteran, short on patience and strong on profanity. At his worst, he was apt to rage and rant like a sore-footed mountain lion. Such as right now, for instance. En route to Logantown, Wyoming, the eastbound had almost finished its crossing of the Rockies and was approaching the west edge of Garvie's Gorge, spanned by the 80 feet long bridge that was the pride and joy of Trans-West's engineers. Ike McGreel, staring ahead, spotted the obstruction and loosed an ear-blistering oath.

"Doyle, take a look!" he ordered the fireman. "If you see what I see, I'll know I ain't dreamin'!"

He was already applying the brakes, when fireman Doyle thrust his head out and squinted ahead. Steel screeched on steel. The caboose and the two Pullman cars shuddered, jolting the passengers in their seats.

1

"I see him too," frowned Doyle. "A rider—just sittin' his animal right there on the tracks."

"Move that damn-blasted critter!" bellowed McGreel, sounding his whistle. "Clear the track!"

But the lone horseman stayed put, sitting a chestnut filly and raising both hands, waving urgently to the engine crew. The locomotive rolled closer before steaming to a halt, and McGreel recognized the rider.

"It's that same pea-brained idiot!" he raged.

"The one they call Crazy Max?" asked Doyle.

"Use your eyes," scowled McGreel. "You've seen him—the last twice he stopped us this side of the gorge."

"Uh huh. Same feller," agreed the fireman.

The conductor and several passengers had climbed down and advanced level with the cabin of the locomotive.

"What the hell, McGreel . . . ?" began the conductor.

"Same feller, Dan," said Doyle.

"Aw, hell!" groaned the conductor. "*No!* Not *him* again!"

"Get rid of him!" ordered McGreel, trembling with fury. "Get him out of my way or, so

2

help me, I'll throw him into the consarned gorge—and his dad-blasted horse after him!"

Two male pasengers thrust themselves to the fore and began questioning the conductor, the while they stared ahead at the horseman blocking the tracks. Their names were Morrison and Kilburn and they were a formidable couple, heavyset, alert-eyed, rigged in town suits, but wearing flat-crowned Stetsons and with the hang of their jackets broken by the bulk of .45's holstered at their right hips. Kilburn, the redhead gnawing on the half-smoked cigar, toted a small valise.

"Won't delay you folks any longer than it takes to move this jasper off the rails," the conductor promised.

"We're three minutes behind schedule already!" boomed McGreel.

"Who is he?" Morrison gruffly challenged. "What does he want anyway? Couldn't be a hold-up. He doesn't show a gun."

"That's Crazy Max from Logantown," the conductor explained. "He's got a fool notion the bridge is gonna fall. This makes the third time this month he's stopped us at Garvie's Gorge."

"Damn fool ought to be locked up," growled Morrison.

3

"Fitch!" The conductor yelled to the horseman. "You're beggin' for a whole mess of trouble! Move clear . . . !"

"Tell the engineer to reverse," begged Max Fitch. "It's about to happen—I warn you! This bridge can't take the weight of the train!"

"The heck it can't!" countered the fireman. "We been crossin' the gorge by way of this here bridge ever since the railroad built her—seven years ago! Twice a week—every week of the year . . . !"

"A structural fault . . ." It seemed Max Fitch enjoyed a better than average command of English. "The stays and cross-beams need reinforcement . . ."

"Who is this galoot anyway?" demanded Kilburn. "A construction engineer—a bridge expert?"

"Well—uh—no," frowned the conductor. "He runs a little livery stable on Colley Road, in Logantown."

"That's all he is—just a stablehand?" Morrison grimaced impatiently. "And he's got the stone-cold nerve to stop a train . . . ?"

"He oughta be locked up!" roared McGreel. "Damn fool claims he had a vision . . . !"

"A what?" frowned Kilburn.

4

"A vision," said the conductor. "Claims he saw the whole thing in a dream—saw the bridge collapse when a train started crossin' . . ." He gesticulated wildly and made to descend from his cabin. "That crazy jackass—I'll break every bone in his body . . . !"

"You get up steam again, Mister Engineer," offered Morrison, crooking a finger at his partner. "My friend and I, we'll take care of the stablehand. Let's go, Webb."

At the conductor's urging, the other passengers returned to the Pullman cars and McGreel climbed back to the footplate, while Morrison and Kilburn strode along the tracks to where the bridge began. There, like the equestrian statues beloved of Civil War heroes, Max Fitch sat his clean-limbed chestnut. He had stopped waving. Now he was still and watchful, his expression a mite apprehensive as the tough-looking passengers advanced on him.

In his 29th year, Maxwell Fitch was slight of build, with sensitive features and a mane of curly dark hair straggling from under the brim of his hat. It was the face of a dreamer, but none of his fellow-citizens of Logantown had ever considered him an intellectual. His instincts were gregarious. He liked people, and he had his practical side, but few locals suspected this. The majority had written him off as an alarmist with a weakness for the melodramatic touch—harmless, provided his warnings were ignored.

"Young feller, you're getting to be a blamed nuisance," accused Morrison. "High time somebody taught you a lesson."

"Move that horse," ordered Kilburn. "Clear the tracks—now!"

"I have to stop that train," Max earnestly explained. "If the engineer attempts a crossing, there'll be a—a massive tragedy—great loss of life—death and destruction . . ."

"I'll bet he strips and runs around the back streets of Logantown," Kilburn remarked to Morrison, "baying like a hound-dog every full moon."

"I'm not exaggerating!" Max protested. "It's all true! I saw it . . . !"

"Yeah, we know," grinned Kilburn. "In a dream."

"Off the horse, dreamer," growled Morrison, seizing a leg.

The prophet protested, but he was no match for Morrison and Kilburn, who hauled him from his mount and dumped him beside the tracks. When he tried to scramble to his feet, Morrison lashed out with a boot and drove him clear across to the edge of the right-of-way, the plank-floored section of the bridge used by horses and wagons. Gasping, his face ashen with pain, Max made another attempt to rise. He almost made it, but Kilburn dashed at him and swung the valise; its edge struck his jaw and he sprawled on his back.

McGreel sounded the whistle. The conductor had returned to his caboose and the eastbound was ready to roll again, but Morrison and his partner were not letting up on their befuddled victim. The chestnut filly had pranced clear of the tracks. Kilburn, chuckling harshly, stood over Max Fitch and jabbed at his ribs with the toe of his boot. Max groaned a protest and began crawling away from him; he had temporarily lost his sense of direction and did not realize he was crawling back onto the tracks. Again McGreel sounded his whistle. Doyle called to Max's assailants, but they were enjoying their work now; cold smiles lit their faces as they watched their victim struggling to regain his feet.

Watching from the side door of his caboose, the conductor heard the clip-clop of hooves and turned to study two more riders. They were moving along beside the tracks, making for the plank walk of the bridge and taking their time, until they spotted Max and his attackers.

In the cabin of the locomotive, Doyle set his shovel down, nudged McGreel and opined,

"We ain't gettin' out of here in a hurry. Here comes more trouble."

"*Now* what?" demaneded McGreel.

"Ike, if I was you, I wouldn't start hollerin' at these two," muttered Doyle.

"Saddlebums, from the looks of 'em," growled McGreel, as the newcomers rode past the locomotive.

"Maybe so," nodded Doyle. "But I sure wouldn't want to tangle with 'em."

One of the riders had called a reprimand to Morrison and Kilburn. He was reining up in front of the engine and dropping to the ground, a burly, broad-shouldered hombre, ruggedly handsome in his well-worn range rig. A battered, sweat-stained Stetson was shoved to the back of his thatch of dark brown hair. The face was sun-tanned and weatherbeaten, heavy-jawed, the jutting underlip suggesting belligerence. To the watching train crew, he certainly sounded belligerent, as he drawled a scathing challenge.

"You heroes need some help maybe? Only two of you to beat up this one puny galoot— you're apt to get weary."

The sarcasm caused Morrison to redden. Unhurriedly, the second drifter cooled his saddle and stood beside his cohort, revealing himself to be all of three inches taller, which made him some six feet six inches, a towering, gangling beanpole. Like his sidekick, he wore range clothes, the rig of the ranch-hand. He was sandy-haired and homely, his blue eyes guileless, never as expressive as the dark eyes of his saddlepard. His mouth was too wide, his ears stuck out and he was lantern jawed. When it came to good looks, Stretch Emerson was no winner, nor was he as nimble-witted as his partner, the wily Larry Valentine. But he made up for these shortcomings; he had other, more important qualities, such as loyalty, a sense of humor and, in time of conflict, a what-the-hell kind of courage allied with brute strength that belied his scrawny physique.

"They sure are brave, huh runt?" he remarked, sizing up Max Fitch's attackers.

"Real heroes," jeered Larry. "As brave as a couple of coyotes cornerin' a prairie chicken."

"Watch it, Tex," scowled Morrison. "Smart talk could win you a fat lip."

"*You* watch it, mister," retorted Stretch. He was grinning, but coldly. "My ol' buddy don't admire to see a man kicked when he's down. You try it one more time—and he's apt to beat your brains out."

"Stand clear of him," ordered Larry, jerking a thumb. "Climb aboard—while you're still able."

"I crave to hear this lame-brain yelp again," Kilburn remarked to Morrison.

Defying Larry's warning, he drew back a boot. Max gasped a plea and back-stepped, and then the Texans were charging, bunching their fists and choosing their adversaries. Larry, rushing Morrison, detoured slightly to buffet Max, shoving him clear. Stretch bore down on Kilburn, who swung at him with the valise. The bag bounced off Stretch's chest without checking his rush. He came on fast, blocked a punch from Kilburn's free fist, then doubled him with a couple of slamming blows to the midriff. As he dropped to his knees, Kilburn

10

made feeble, wheezing sounds, saliva dripping from his sagging mouth.

Morrison met Larry's rush with a left to the jaw and a right to the ear, and neither punch distressed the veteran brawler. The jaw-blow skinned Morrison's knuckles. The other punch bloodied Larry's left ear, but Larry didn't appear to notice. His own left flashed out rock-hard and piston-fast, slamming to Morrison's chin, jerking his head back, dazing him. Glassy-eyed and limp, Morrison buckled at the knees and went down in an untidy, mumbling heap. For a moment Larry stood over him, hoping he would rise and resume the hassle. He didn't.

"Kinda disappointin'," Stretch commented.

"Ain't that the truth?" agreed Larry. He turned to face the engine and call to the crew. "If these galoots belong on your train, you better pick 'em up and throw 'em up aboard."

Abruptly, the Texans lost interest in their adversaries. While Doyle and the conductor descended and came forward to help Morrison and Kilburn to their feet, the drifters stepped away from the tracks, Larry grasping Max's arm and walking him over to where the filly awaited, Stretch leading his and Larry's mounts by their reins.

11

Doyle darted a covert glance at them, as he supported the still-wheezing Kilburn, helping him along to the first passenger car. Kilburn seemed oblivious to everything except the valise; he clung to it, as the conductor helped him into the passenger car.

"I can't watch!" gasped Max Fitch.

He stood with shoulders bowed, eyes closed, hands clamped to his ear, while the eastbound resumed its journey, steaming onto the bridge. The Texans rolled and lit cigarettes and watched the train rumble and clatter across to the east lip of the gorge without mishap. No shuddering of timbers or buckling of metal, no ominous movement of the causeway, nothing vaguely resembling a catastrophe. Whistle tooting, smoke puffing from its stack, the locomotive hauled its tender, caboose and two passenger cars on across the wind-swept mesa toward the downgrade that led to Logantown.

Larry shrugged, lit his cigarette from the match scratched by Stretch and calmly asked Max,

"How come you didn't want to watch?"

"Not much to see anyway," drawled Stretch. "Just one little old train rollin' 'cross the bridge."

12

Gingerly, Max turned to stare after the train. His gaze dropped to the timber and steel structure spanning the gorge and, with a sigh of relief, he mumbled,

"Not this time—but soon. These people were lucky. The next train—who knows?"

"You want to tell us what it's all about?" asked Larry. "Why were those jaspers beatin' up on you? Why'd the train stall this side of the gorge anyway?"

"Young feller, you don't have to answer them questions," Stretch hastened to assure him. "You don't have to tell us a thing."

"Talk for yourself," countered Larry.

"Listen now, runt," protested Stretch. "We promised ourselves we'd find the first town east of the mountains and . . ."

"That'll be Logantown," interjected Max.

"And gamble a little, drink a mite, sleep on soft beds a couple days," finished Stretch. He added, with heavy emphasis, "And mind our own damn business."

"If this hombre wants to talk about why he got roughed up, I can't stop him," Larry pointed out. "It's a free country."

"You'd hear about it anyway, if you're visiting Logantown," Max said glumly. "Oh,

13

sure. You'd be bound to run into some wiseacre who'd want to talk about Crazy Max."

"Who?" frowned Stretch, taking a pace backward.

"My name is Max Fitch, and that's what they call me," said Max.

"Crazy?" prodded Larry.

"Because . . ." Max grimaced uncomfortably, "because I think I have second sight—or something. I can't explain it very well." He turned to stare away at the snow-capped peaks to the north. "I see things in my dreams. And later—sometimes—the dream comes true."

"Just sometimes?" challenged Larry.

"That's what makes it difficult for me," said Max. "My predictions aren't always accurate."

"He talks educated," Stretch observed.

"Let's not hold that aginst him," suggested Larry.

"Some folks claim I should have used my education to better advantage, but they just don't understand," said Max. "I'm studying veterinary science by correspondence. I've always like animals and understood them, so why shouldn't I run a livery stable? When I finish my studies, I'll be able to expand the business and . . ."

14

"What's this veter—vetery . . . ?" began Stretch.

"Means he's studyin' how to be a horse-doctor," explained Larry. He delved into his saddlebag and produced the dwindling liquor supply of the Lone Star Hellions, a half-pint of rye. "Max, you better take a slug of this."

"Just a short one." Max accepted the bottle, took a modest swig and returned it to Larry, who fed himself a stiff one before passing the bottle to his partner. "They hurt me, but I don't feel so bad now. The ribs ache . . ." He shrugged philosophically. "Well, it's happened before and it'll happen again. People distrust what they don't understand—and few people understand me."

"You dreamed somethin' about this bridge?" demanded Larry.

"I saw it so clearly," Max declared. "The entire causeway sagging—a train plunging into the gorge . . ."

"Well," said Stretch, "it didn't happen that way, did it?"

"Not *this* time," frowned Max.

"Still think it's gonna happen?" prodded Larry.

"I'd rather be wrong," Max fervently assured

15

him. "I'd rather the whole community laughed me to scorn—than for such a tragedy to occur —the way I saw it in my dream." He shook his head sadly. "Did I say dream? Nightmare would be a better word for it."

"Max, you think that bridge is safe for us to ride across?" asked Stretch, winking at Larry.

"I saw no horses in the dream," said Max, as he remounted the chestnut.

The Texans stepped up to leather, Larry straddling his rangy sorrel, Stretch swinging astride the sprightly pinto. As they walked the animals level with the railroad tracks and on to the right-of-way, the young livery-owner pointed out,

"You have the advantage of me. I didn't think to ask your names."

"Valentine," said Larry. "Friends call me Larry. This beanpole sidekick of mine is Woodville Eustace Emerson. Anybody calls him Woodville, he's just beggin' for a busted jaw. You want to stay sociable with him, you call him Stretch."

"Larry and Stretch," mused Max. "Those names have a familiar ring."

In silence, the three ambled their mounts across the bridge. Every foot of the way, Max

16

kept his eyes downcast, studying the walls of the gorge and its floor 100 feet below, the gleaming surface of a tributary of the Sweetwater flowing to the south. Then, when the crossing ended, he transferred his attention to his rough-hewn benefactors and reflected,

"They'll be the same two. They'd *have* to be. There couldn't be two other trouble-shooters called Larry and Stretch."

In frontier towns, bartenders, lawmen and barbers heard snatches of talk, rumors, tall tales of deeds of daring. And, if those towns happened to boast a newspaper, there was a better than even chance some of the wilder rumors, some of the taller tales, would end up in print. Max realized now that these were the adventurers whose exploits he'd heard discussed since the days of his youth, the same Larry and Stretch who had been thrown together during the early days of the Civil War and had stayed together these past eighteen years, always on the drift, always in trouble of one kind or another.

In their own rough fashion, the Texas Trouble-Shooters were law-abiding; unfortunately their fashion was a mite too rough for the sensitivities of duly appointed county sheriffs and town marshals. Lawmen distrusted them almost as much as did the lawless. They had become the sworn enemies of all denizens of the owlhoot camps and were forever warring against stage-robbers, rustlers, bank-bandits, homicidal gunmen and every other breed of badman infesting the wild frontiers west of the Mississippi. And, to the consternation of badge-toters everywhere, they fought the lawless according to their own what-the-hell code, with scant regard for due process. It was a matter of record that they were equally disrespectful of Federal law officers, the Pinkerton Agency, the US Treasury and the US Army. Authority in any shape or form seemed to irritate these raffish nomads.

"Max . . ." The taller Texan intruded on his reverie, "you ever had any dreams that did come true?"

"Quite a few—and it can be downright frightening," sighed Max. "A few months back, for instance, I tried to warn Mayor Ashworth against taking a buggy ride out to the K and G ranch. Just the night before, I saw the whole thing in a dream—the buggy overturned—the mayor lying unconscious with his head bloody . . ."

"He wouldn't listen to you, huh?" challenged Larry.

"I did my best to make him understand," muttered Max. "A big crowd gathered outside City Hall. You see, I kept barring his way, standing in front of his team, refusing to let him pass."

He grimaced, suddenly embarrassed by his memories. "After a while, Mayor Ashworth lost his temper and took a swing at me with his whip."

"And . . . ?"

"Well—he missed me . . ."

"That's good."

". . . but struck his team—and they bolted."

"That's bad."

"At the corner of Main and Colley, the mayor's rig skidded. A wheel hit a water trough and the buggy overturned. Mayor Ashworth was thrown clear, but he suffered a slight head injury."

"So the dream came true that time," grinned Larry.

"Almost as though I *made* it come true," fretted Max. "Who knows? If I'd stayed away from him, he might've reached the K and G safely." He shook his head impatiently. "I'd as soon not talk about it any more."

"Okay by us," shrugged Larry.

"I owe you my thanks for protecting me against those passengers," said Max.

"Forget it," grunted Stretch.

"I'd like to show my appreciation," said Max. "At least let me offer you the hospitality of the Happy Haven."

"How's that again?" frowned Larry.

"I mean hospitality for your horses," Max explained. "Happy Haven—that's what I call my stable. There'll be a couple of comfortable stalls for your animals in my barn for as long as you stay in Logantown."

"That won't be long," said Larry. "Two-three days at most. Every once in a while we crave a little town-livin', but the cravin' soon wears off."

"Itchy feet," Stretch told Max. "We like to keep movin'."

"Yes, the wanderlust." Max nodded understandingly as he studied them again. Sitting their horses in the slumped posture of the veteran range rider, they looked relaxed and durable, uncommonly healthy, considering the score or more pitched battles they had figured in these past few years. Impulsively he remarked, "It's hard to believe." They raised their eyebrows in casual enquiry. "I mean— all the stories I've heard about the Lone Star Hellions. You look so ordinary. No offense, but you don't seem very aggressive right now."

"We ain't special," Stretch modestly assured him. "Just a couple do-right Texans tryin' to keep our noses clean. If we never run into another hassle, why, that'll be soon enough for us."

"Amen to that," said Larry. "Hey, Max, you a gamblin' man?"

"No," said Max. "I get nervous. The atmosphere in a saloon when men play poker or throw dice for high stakes . . ." He shook his head and frowned uneasily. "All the tension—men holding their breath while a card is dealt or the dice thrown or the wheel turned." Sadly he confided, "I don't enjoy the tension. If I had my way, life would be simple and quiet. There'd be peace—every man living in harmony with his neighbor . . ." He broke off, staring sidelong at Larry, but with a far-away expression in his eyes. Matching his stare, Larry got the impression the dreamer was seeing through and beyond him. "Mister Valentine . . ."

"Make it Larry," offered Larry.

"Larry, if you're determined to gamble . . ." began Max.

"It never yet hurt his nerves," grinned Stretch.

"You should play the wheel tonight," said Max. "I just . . ." He paused, half-closed his eyes and raised a hand to his brow, "I saw it —just briefly. You were winning . . ."

"Hey, he's dreamin'!" chuckled Stretch. "Wide awake—and dreamin' out loud!"

"I'm not joking," said Max. "There's a roulette game at the Wheel Of Fortune—Phil Crane's saloon. Larry, you don't have to heed my advice . . ."

"And if I *want* to heed it?" asked Larry.

"I don't believe you'd win at poker or any other card game tonight," said Max. "But, at roulette . . ." He shrugged and stared ahead to where the east rim of the mesa dipped toward the foothills and, studying him covertly, Larry couldn't decide if he were over-confident, apprehensive, sad or happy. With an odd character like Max Fitch, it was hard to tell. "Roulette would be best for you."

22

"You got any other notions, boy?" prodded Stretch. "About, for instance, what numbers he ought to play."

"Even numbers, I think," said Max. "I could answer your question more confidently, Stretch, if I could see the wheel."

"You'll see the wheel," Stretch cheerfully promised. "Tonight we're takin' you to the Wheel of Fortune and you're gonna tell us where to lay our bets."

"You'd risk your money, just to find out if I'm clairvoyant?" asked Max.

"We got nothin' to better to do," shrugged Larry.

He was interested in people, in humanity in general and, most particularly, in the off-beat folk, the unconventionals, the out-of-the-rut frontier types who refused to conform. Max Fitch, in Larry's opinion, was one of the gentle people and out of his element in any rough Wyoming cattle-town, though his ambition made sense; the frontier needed good veterinarians. Men like Max could so easily be hurt, he reflected. Not just hurt. Battered, lost in the shuffle, trampled underfoot, snuffed out. There was no belligerence in Max. When those two arrogant jaspers off the train had started crowding him, Max hadn't known how to defend himself, hadn't as much as lifted a hand against them.

He voiced the thought in his mind, as they began the descent to the foothills.

"Maxie boy, I don't know how you've lasted this long."

"Funny," said Max. "I was thinking exactly the same about you and Stretch."

From the observation platform of the first Pullman car, Bart Morrison and Webb Kilburn studied the county seat and its environs. The eastbound rumbled through Logantown's outskirts and on toward the depot at Main Street's south end, so the newcomers were offered a panoramic view of the town— sprawling, sun-baked, dusty and false-fronted —and the land beyond; prairie and cattle graze to the northeast, the high peaks of the Rockies to the west and, twenty-five miles south of the Sweetwater, more of the soaring grandeur of the Continental Divide.

"Big town," Morrison remarked. "Four banks," Crane said.

"The other three don't matter a damn,"

muttered Kilburn. "For us, it has to be the Settlers National—the biggest."

"All that beautiful paper," drawled Morrison, dropping his gaze to the small valise. "Worth no more than its weight in newspaper —but it's gonna make us rich."

"The pictures," Kilburn said with a sly grin, "are prettier than you'd seen in any news-paper."

"How about this Crane?" Morrison demanded. "How far can we trust him?"

"All the way," said Kilburn. "Like I told you before, I worked with Phil a long time back. He's a smart one, Bart, and plenty useful. If he says he's figured a way to work the switch, you can bet it's sure-fire."

"It better be sure-fire," retorted Morrison. "With this kind of deal, you get only one chance."

"We can count on Phil Crane," Kilburn assured him, as the train reached the depot. "We'll go find his saloon rightaway." He scowled and felt at his midriff. "My belly's stopped aching. I could use a drink."

Toting their bags, they descended to the depot platform and made for the main stem. It was mid-week, but there were more than a few ranch-hands in town, rubbing shoulders with townfolk and transients strolling the broad and dusty thoroughfare. From the second floor galleries of the saloons and joy-houses nearest the railroad depot, gaudily-gowned women called greetings to the new arrivals; a blowsy blonde waved to Kilburn and smiled an invitation. He flashed her a grin and doffed his hat, playing the gallant, while Morrison muttered a warning.

"We're here on business—the biggest deal we ever pulled. So don't let's get side-tracked." They were almost half-way along the main street when he nudged Kilburn and remarked, "There it is."

"Only bank in town with a vault," mused Kilburn, scanning the imposing facade of the Settlers National Bank. "Only bank that needs a vault."

"Because they hold more cash than any other bank in Logantown," nodded Morrison.

They entered the next block and sighted the brightly-painted wagon wheel and the red-on-white lettering of a shingle identifying their destination, Phil Crane's Wheel Of Fortune Saloon, Logantown's biggest and gaudiest.

A few moments after moving into the

26

barroom, they were hailed by the proprietor from his private table to the right of the staircase, a vantagepoint from whence Phil Crane could keep an eye on every game of chance, as well as the bar and the main entrance. He was a lean one, well-groomed and handsome, though his taste in haberdashery was a mite too effeminate for Morrison's liking. The dark hair was slicked down with pomade and graying slightly at the temples. The eyes were bright blue and alert and, when he smiled, he smiled only with his mouth; the eyes stayed alert and humorless.

They approached Crane's table in response to his welcoming gesture, Kilburn grinning expansively, Morrison thoughtfully eyeing Crane's companion, a generously-curved blonde in a tightfitting gown of deep green silk.

"Good to see you, Webb." Crane's voice was soft and almost devoid of expression. "Welcome to Logantown. It's been a long time, Webb." He offered a well-manicured hand. "And this'll be your partner?"

"Bart Morrison," offered Kilburn. "told you about him in my letter."

"I never took kindly to Webb writing you," Morrison bluntly declared, as he shook hands with the saloonkeeper. "Putting that kind of a deal on paper and mailing it . . ."

"Kind of like mailing a can of blasting powder and hoping nobody'll light a match near it," nodded Crane. "I felt the same way, Morrison, when I answered Webb's letter. But that's all over now. I burned his letter. I'm sure he burned mine . . ."

"You could bet your life on that," chuckled Kilburn, as he seated himself.

Morrison set the bags down and took the other vacant chair; he was studying the woman again. Crane snapped his fingers. A barkeep fetched a bottle and two extra glasses, and Crane waited for him to return to the bar before performing introductions.

"You've heard me speak of them," he told the woman.

"Was that smart?" challenged Morrison.

"I have no secrets from her," drawled Crane. "She knows the whole score . . ."

"The hell she does," frowned Morrison.

"When it's all over, she'll become Mrs. Phil Crane." The saloonkeeper placed a hand on her bare shoulder. "Gents, say hallo to Rose Dawes. And don't get nervous about her. She's tight-mouthed—knows how to keep a secret."

28

The woman spoke for the first time. Her voice was as soft as Crane's, and husky, with a hint of boredom and world-weariness.

"Was the train-trip all that rough?" she challenged the newcomers. "You two look like you wrassled a wild bull."

Morrison turned red. Kilburn poured himself a stiff shot of bourbon and swigged at it thirstily.

"Ran into a little trouble," Morrison said curtly.

"Where?" demanded Crane.

"Other side of the bridge," said Morrison, shrugging impatiently. "I think they call it Garvie's Gorge . . ."

"Why, sure," nodded Crane. "That's the only important bridge hereabouts." He grinned again and traded glances with Rose Dawes. "Don't tell me the train was delayed at the gorge—again?"

"By a dreamy-eyed jasper that rides a chestnut?" prodded Rose. As Morrison nodded, she smiled blandly. "Well, well, well. Crazy Max is at it again."

"But Fitch couldn't land a punch on the likes of you or Webb," protested Crane.

"It wasn't Fitch did this to us," scowled Kilburn. "Couple strangers showed up."

"Saddletramps," grunted Morrison. "They got lucky is all." Pointedly he reminded Crane, "We have more important things to discuss."

"You'll be using the room next to mine—for the short time you're here," said Crane, as he got to his feet. "We'll take you up and get you settled in." Nodding affably to Kilburn, he added, "Bring the bottle."

In the room adjoining Crane's office, Morrison stowed the bags in a corner, all but the small valise which he placed on one of the beds. Rose Dawes took her ease in a chair by the open window, watching, but showing no great interest. Crane, standing by the bed and puffing on a cigar, gestured for Morrison to reveal the valise's contents.

"Let's see the merchandise, Morrison. I'm curious, wondering if it's as good as Webb claims."

"It's good," Morrison assured him, as he snapped the catches. "Better than anything you've seen—outside of the genuine article."

He raised the lid of the valise to reveal the contents—banknotes—neatly bundled and tightly packed. But for one very important

30

detail, Crane might have believed the valise held a fortune, a king's ransom. He whistled softly.

"Got to agree with you, Morrison," he muttered.

"Yeah, sure," grinned Morrison. "I knew you'd be impressed." He delved into the valise, slid a bill from one of the bundles and offered it for Crane's inspection. The saloonkeeper felt it, held it up to the light and studied it with great intensity. "You're looking for flaws," Morrison pointed out. "The average citizen doesn't."

"And yet, when the first printing began circulating, there was a hullabaloo in Portland," frowned Crane. "Treasury men ran your old friends to ground in no time at all. The ring was broken up."

"Two of us got away," countered Morrison.

"With the plates," grinned Kilburn.

Crane returned the banknote, squinted into the valise and observed,

"Bills of every denomination! Got to hand it to you, Morrison, You've spared no effort."

"It's a one-time deal," said Morrison. "Instead of changing a few bills here and there, taking months to show a profit and risking arrest all the time, we get rid of the whole bundle in one operation."

"How much in the bag?" asked Rose Dawes, without turning her head.

Kilburn named the amount. Crane whistled again, grinned mirthlessly and remarked,

"If it were the real stuff, we'd be the richest men in Wyoming."

"It's close enough to the real stuff," insisted Morrison. "I mean close enough to fool everybody."

"Not for long," said Crane. "But long enough for us to disappear from the territory. We'll all be long gone by the time the bank authorities get wise." Grinning at Kilburn, nodding reassuringly, he held up two fingers. "Two days, Webb. We can travel quite a way in two days."

"What two days?" demanded Morrison.

"Saturday and Sunday," said Crane. "The banks will be closing Friday afternoon. They don't open again until . . ."

"I know what time the banks operate," Morrison said impatiently. "Crane, are you saying we can switch the stuff Friday night? Hell! Today's Wednesday."

"It can be done," Crane promised. "In a little

while I'll show you how. It will be quiet, Morrison. No violence. No bloodshed. No threats. After all . . ." He chuckled softly and winked at the woman, "you could hardly say we're planning a bank robbery. It's more . . ." He searched his mind for the right words. "Well, let's call it an exchange of funds—a little money-changing."

"Money-changing!" Kilburn guffawed and flopped into a chair. "Hey, that's good. That's damn funny."

"We have only one bank that carries such heavy weight deposits," Crane told Morrison. "But that's okay. In that one bank . . ."

"Meaning the Settlers National," said Morrison.

"Meaning the Settlers National," nodded Crane. "In that one bank we have a contact, a man who'll be ready and willing to co-operate." He fished out a gold watch and glanced at it. "You'll meet him in a little while, Morrison. He always comes straight after the bank closes." Jerking a thumb, he calmly explained, "He wants Rose—and Rose has been hinting she's available. His name is Taflin, Jay Taflin, and she's got him eating out of her hand."

2

THOUGH it had become Logantown's busiest bank, the Settlers National had only a two-man staff. The manager, venerable Aaron Hinchley, was a veteran of the business, but durable, still spry in his advanced 50's and able to do double duty as first cashier and bookkeeper.

That afternoon, just before quitting the bank with Jay Taflin, he paused in the street doorway to study the mahogany-topped counter, the well-swept floor and spotlessly clean windows, Taflin's desk with inkwell and papers neatly arranged, the polished knob of the door to his private office and, away to the right, the strong-room door with the combination lock.

"A place for everything—and everything in its place," he remarked. "Looks fine, doesn't it, Taflin? I think we can pride ourselves on running the tidiest, safest bank in all of Logan County."

"You should be very proud, Mister Hinchley," said the cashier. He was forty, florid and squatly-built, running to fat, but oblivious to his shortcomings. Outwardly diffident, Jay Taflin indulged many a secret conceit; he considered himself to be Hinchley's superior in wit and good looks, and a lady-killer to boot. During business hours, however, he was careful to accord his chief all due respect. "I'm sure Mister Glynn will be favorably impressed."

"A great day for the Logantown branch," smiled Hinchley, as they moved out to the sidewalk. He closed and locked the door, pocketed the key and glanced downtown toward the railroad depot. "And a personal tribute to me. I'm trying to be modest, Taflin. But, damnitall, after twenty years of loyal service to the Settlers National, I think I've earned recognition, acknowledgement, maybe a word of praise."

"You'll get all that, and more, on Friday night," Taflin predicted. "It should be quite a function, Mister Hinchley. The manager of the Logantown branch playing host to the president of the company . . ."

"Not just a dinner—a banquet," declared Hinchley. "I've reserved the entire dining room of the Grand Western, spent a small fortune on new gowns for Louisa and her mother and ordered a five-course meal—with champagne."

"I understand Casper Glynn is fond of making speeches."

"Well, that's his privilege, Taflin. After all, he founded the Settlers National chain. And I don't mind if he bends our ears." Hinchley grinned indulgently. "All in a good cause, Taflin. At my age, a man values such tributes."

"Twenty years in the banking business," nodded Taflin. "Ten years a branch manager for the Settlers National, and no bank managed by you has ever been robbed. I certainly congratulate you, Mister Hinchley. You've earned the gold medal, the plaque and the illuminated scroll."

"I surely have," agreed Hinchley. "And I thank you for those kind words, Taflin."

He nodded so-long to the cashier and strolled away toward the Grand Western, the hotel favored by Logan County's upper crust. On the second floor gallery, every day at this hour, the manager of the Settlers National was wont to socialize with such notable civic leaders as Mayor Gus Ashworth, County Sheriff Todd Waterbury and Marcus Drew, who owned the Grand Western and a generous portion of the local real estate.

Jay Taflin turned and made off in the

36

opposite direction. His destination was the barroom of the Wheel Of Fortune, where he hoped to find his favorite percentage-woman at liberty, able to spare him a little of her time. His florid face was impassive; he had learned to conceal impatience, his contempt for the snowy-haired banker who had been his amiable boss these past three years. After all, the Settlers National paid his salary. To insult Hinchley to his face was a luxury he just couldn't afford.

Entering the Wheel Of Fortune a short time later, he was elated to find the beautiful blonde seated alone at the piano over by the dance floor, boredly strumming chords. As he headed in that dirction, his movements were followed with interest by Morrison and Crane, watching from the top of the stairs.

"There he is now," offered the saloonkeeper.

"Well . . ." Morrison clamped a cigar between his teeth, "I guess you can't judge a book by its cover. Just looking at this Taflin, I wouldn't trust him any further than I could throw him."

"He'll deliver," grinned Crane. "For a chance at Rose, He'd betray his own mother."

"A bank cashier," mused Morrison.

"You have to admit this is the easiest way,"

37

said Crane. "Who better to work the switch, than an employee of the bank? Without Taflin's help, the job would be more complicated."

"We're gonna have to trust him—with the whole bundle," Morrison pointed out.

"*We* can trust him, but I wouldn't say the same of the Settlers National," drawled Crane. "A few months ago, while he was hung over and needing sympathy, I fed Taflin a hair of the dog. He became very confidential, you know what I mean? Let me in on a secret."

"Something important?"

"From our point of view, yes. But nothing very spectacular. All he said was he'd been in trouble with the law before he came to Logantown."

"Well, that's something. Anything else you can use against him—outside of the woman?"

"Oh, sure. I let him run up quite a tab here."

"Listen, if he's a drunk . . ."

"No. He hardly ever drinks too much. He ran up his tab at my poker tables, and that was okay by me. Always had a hunch it might prove useful—a bank cashier in debt to me."

"All right." Morision nodded curtly. "Give your woman the high sign. Have her fetch him up here, and then we'll see how he takes to the idea." On an afterthought, he added, "He'd better take to it, Crane."

"I already thought of that," Crane calmly declared. "He buys it—or he has a fatal accident."

"He'd know too much," frowned Morrison. "He's with us, Crane, or . . ."

"Or he's dead," finished Crane. He smiled coldly and muttered an assurance. "Don't worry about it, Morrison. These things can be arranged."

He followed Morrison, after crooking a finger at Rose Dawes, who was pretending to listen to her paunchy admirer, but keeping an eye on the gallery. As the saloonkeeper moved away from the gallery rail, she turned on the piano-stool, stared into Taflin's face and placed a hand on his.

"I wonder if you really mean it," she murmured. "You make a mighty pretty speech, Jay, but I wonder if you mean all you say."

"Believe it," he breathed. "There's nothing you could name—nothing I wouldn't do for you . . ."

"Supposing I told you I was onto something?"

"On to—something?"

"Something big, Jay. We'd end up rich, and then we could do all the things you've been talking about. We'd leave Wyoming—leave the west—together . . ."

"Together?" He eyed her eagerly. "You'd do it, Rose? You'd—come with me?"

"And stay with you," she softly assured him, "for as long as you wanted me."

"I've been wanting you from the first moment I laid eyes on you," he muttered.

"I know," she nodded. "I've felt you looking at me. You got heavy eyes, Jay. Real heavy eyes."

He was silent a moment, his gaze shifting to the late afternoon trade, the towners lining the bar and converging on the games of chance.

"It'd be risky?" he asked.

"Not for you," she whispered. "You're a cool one, Jay. I understand you, and I know you won't let us down."

"Us?"

"I told you it's big. We couldn't handle it alone. But one thing you can count on. Your share will be a bonanza, more cash than you ever saw before."

"I work in a bank—remember?"

"Sure, Jay. You've handled thousands, and

how did it feel? You enjoy stowing it back in the vault every day when the bank closes?"

"Who else is in it?"

"I can't tell you that till I know where you stand."

"You know where I stand, Rose. I'm with you. There's nothing I wouldn't do—*nothing*."

"All right, sweetheart, you've made your point." She laughed huskily, rose from the stool and linked her arm through his. "Let's go talk to Phil and the others."

"I guess Crane'd be mixed into it," he muttered, as they moved across to the stairs. "But who're these other jaspers?"

"You don't have to be leery of them," she assured him. "They're professionals. They're supplying most of the equipment, so they'll draw the biggest share of the loot. I guess that's fair enough."

"There'll still be plenty for you and me, huh Rose?" he challenged.

"Plenty of everything," she murmured.

She led him along the gallery, past the office and up to the next door, then knocked. Crane opened the door, showed Taflin a genial grin and asked,

"Are we dealing him in?"

"He's in," smiled Rose. "You can count on Jay."

"You thirsty, Taflin?" Crane clapped a friendly hand to the cashier's shoulder and drew him into the room. The woman followed, closing and locking the door behind her. "Got some fine bourbon here. Only the best for my partners." Morrison and Kilburn, perched on the edge of their beds, traded wary nods with the new arrival. The window was closed and the shade lowered. On the table nearest the window, Kilburn had placed the small valise. "Rest of the outfit, Taflin. That's Morrison and the other one is Kilburn."

"My pleasure," said Taflin. He accepted a drink and a cigar, seated himself beside Rose on the sofa and eyed the newcomers expectantly. "All right, gents, you want to talk about it now?"

"It has to be now," muttered Kilburn. "Phil says—and we agree—we ought to be finished by midnight Friday. That'll give us a whole two days to put some distance between us and Logantown. We could be far west of the Wyoming border before your boss starts wailing."

"The idea of Aaron Hinchley wailing . . ."

Taflin grinned eagerly. "I like that fine, gents. I've had my bellyful of that smug old penny-pincher."

"Crane tells me the vault at the Settlers National has a combination lock," said Morrison. "You know the combination?" Taflin nodded slowly. "All right, mister, don't get any wrong ideas. This is no regular grab we're planning. Nothing like it has ever been tried before."

"Planning on emptying the vault, aren't you?" challenged Taflin. "That's not exactly an original idea. It's been done before."

"Not the way we're doing it, friend," drawled Kilburn.

"Emptying that vault will be your chore, Taflin," said Morrison. "And we're gonna make it easy for you."

"How?" demanded Taflin.

"When you've finished your chore, the vault won't *look* empty," explained Morrison. "For every bundle of bills you take out, you'll leave another in its place."

"You mean . . . ?" began Taflin.

"I mean we're gonna compensate the Settlers National," Morrison told him. He grinned mirthlessly as he added, "Temporarily at least."

"It'll be easier for Jay to understand," suggested Crane, "if you show him the merchandise."

"Go ahead," offered Morrison, nodding to the valise. "Help yourself."

Taflin hesitated a moment, then got to his feet and stood by the table, staring down at the valise. He snapped the catches, raised the lid and swore softly. With the practised skill of the veteran cashier, he removed one of the bundles, placed it on the tabletop and riffled through it. He slid a bill from the bundle and inspected it with great care, then crumpled it into a ball and smoothed it out again.

"Outside of the real thing, you'll never see better," Kilburn assured him.

"A few flaws in the art work," Taflin observed. "But the color is damn near perfect. And the paper . . ." He crumpled another bill. "I won't ask how you came by it. I don't need to know." Abruptly, he returned the samples to the valise, closed it and resumed his seat. "All right, you can deal me in."

"A four-way pay-off," said Crane. "You and Rose share a quarter . . ."

"I'm taking the greatest risk. My share ought to be bigger," frowned Taflin.

44

"Don't try hustling us, Taflin," warned Morrison. "We could play this game in any other town. All we need is a fat bank and a greedy cashier."

"We've dealt you in anyway," Crane reminded Taflin. "And I'm being generous— writing off your gambling debt to the Wheel Of Fortune. Get this straight, Taflin. There'll be no turning back. From here on, you follow our orders. As for your cut . . ." He grinned wryly, "you're doing fine—sharing twenty-five percent with Rose."

"I've known jaspers who'd give their eye-teeth for such a chance," declared Kilburn, with an admiring glance at the blonde woman.

"Webb and Morrison supplied the merchandise, so they split fifty percent," said Crane. "The fourth quater is mine."

"Starting tomorrow morning, you're gonna smuggle the stuff into the bank," said Morrison.

"I can do that," nodded Taflin.

"Got a place you can hide it?" demanded Kilburn.

"My desk," said Taflin. "The old man would never look in there."

"Friday afternoon, he'll close up earlier than

45

usual?" asked Crane. "It's no secret he's gonna be honored by the boss of the whole shebang—Casper Glynn himself—president of the Settlers National. Glynn's arriving on the afternoon train."

"And Hinchley will be right there to meet him," said Taflin. "Right there at the depot, along with his wife and daughter and the mayor and half-dozen aldermen. But the bank won't close until the usual time."

"You'll have the place to yourself," grinned Kilburn. "Couldn't be easier, huh Bart?"

"Are we making it plain enough, Taflin?" challenged Morrison. "All you have to do is change the fake dinero for the real stuff."

"It adds up to quite a bundle," frowned Taflin. "I wouldn't want to tote a valise or a carpetbag out of the bank when I close up Friday. Somebody'd be bound to notice—and to remember. I mean later, when the panic starts."

"Wear a duster Friday," advised Morrison. "Stow the cash in your pockets, in your hat, inside your shirt. A duster is mighty effective camouflage."

"From the bank, you come straight here as

usual," said Crane. "We'll be waiting for you —right here in this very room."

"All but Webb," said Morrison. "He'll be close by when you lock up."

"Keeping an eye on me?" challenged Taflin.

"Insurance," Morrison said bluntly.

"Just thinking of your welfare, friend," grinned Kilburn, "and your reputation."

"You might get trampled by a runaway team between here and the Settlers National," drawled Crane. "What is kindly old Sheriff Waterbury gonna think of you, when they search your carcase at the funeral parlor and find all that dinero?"

"It'll be better if Webb tags you after you quit the bank," said Morrison.

"In other words, you don't trust me," accused Taflin. "You're afraid I'd grab the first horse I see and make a run for it."

"I'm sure we can rely on Jay," smiled Rose.

"Insurance," repeated Morrison. "When he walks out of that bank Friday afternoon, Taflin will be toting a lot of temptation."

"There'll be no double-cross," said Taflin. "I'll come straight here for the pay-off."

"I guarantee you will," chuckled Kilburn.

"Any questions, Taflin?" asked Crane.

"Just one," said Taflin, turning to stare at Rose. "How soon can we quit the territory—Rose and me?"

"Just as soon as you want, Jay honey," she murmured.

"I'd need to be a long way from Logantown by Monday morning," declared Taflin. "We have no way of guessing how soon the panic will start, and I want to be long gone before the first fake bill is brought back to the bank."

"We could be on our way Saturday morning," Rose suggested. "I'll rent a buggy and we'll let folks think we're riding out to Quill's Bend for a picnic. Soon as we're clear of town, we'll turn west and head for the mountains."

"That's fine by me," muttered Taflin. "And —the rest of you?"

"I stay put," said Crane. "Why should I run? I can afford to hang around, at least long enough to sell the Wheel Of Fortune."

"You two?" prodded Taflin, frowning at Morrison.

"There'll be a westbound train passing through Friday night, Crane says" drawled Morrison. "We'll be on it."

"Sounds okay," Taflin decided. "Everybody

48

gets clear. Hinchley opens up on schedule Monday morning and by then, Rose and I will be across the border and on our way to Oregon." He took the blonde woman's hand and eyed her expectantly. "Oregon okay by you, Rose?"

"For a starter," she murmured. "But California would be better."

"Oregon or California," he invited. "You name it, Rose. Whatever you say is just fine by me."

For ten more minutes they discussed their plan for the most unique bank robbery in Wyoming's history, and Jay Taflin had never known such excitement, such happy anticipation. His need to hold Aaron Hinchley up to ridicule was as great as his need to possess Rose Dawes. With every passing month, his contempt for the jovial, snow-haired banker had increased, his well-concealed dislike had grown to cold hatred. Jay Taflin's greatest handicap was his capacity for resentment; he had let it get the better of him time and time again. He lacked the patience, the cool head and steady nerve needed for high-stake poker—or any other game of chance—yet he gambled constantly, ineptly, rashly, always resenting the seeming ease with which his adversaries won.

Hinchley was in that category. A winner, though never a gambler. Hinchley had achieved his position of trust with the Settlers National and the respect of the bank's clients through his devotion to their interests and a willingness to work hard, to stay at his desk long hours after closing time. And, off duty, he socialized with the lowly as well as with those citizens who, like himself, lived in fine homes on Rico Hill. So everybody loved and admired the quick-smiling old banker with the silver-knobbed cane, the beaver hat always at an angle on the snowy thatch, the gait always slow and majestic, indicating the manager of the Settlers National was conferring an honor on Logantown just by treading its sidewalks.

"One thing you got to say for old Aaron—he's quality—real high class."

This tribute was often voiced by Hinchley's contemporary, the pudgy, aging and affable Sheriff Todd Waterbury. And, every time he heard his boss so described, Jay Taflin seethed and simmered, his resentment maintained at fever heat, though concealed behind his impassive mask. Had he but realized it, his resentment, his well-sustained hatred of a genial employer, was a proof of his own imaturity. In recruiting Jay Taflin to their cause, Phil Crane and his cohorts had made a serious error of judgement.

There were other men of Logan County inclined to make rash decisions, and four of them were approaching the county seat from the east at about the same time that Max Fitch led Larry and Stretch along Main Street toward the corner of Colley Road. Their leader, boss of the B-Bar ranch, was Al Burchell, a hefty, trigger-tempered redhead who had one quality in common with Jay Taflin, a capacity for resentment. When it came to toting a grudge, the beefy Burchell was an expert; he really worked at it.

Some five minutes before the arrival of the four B-Bar men, Max and his new friends walked their horses into the Happy Haven barn, half-way along Colley Road. On duty was Max's only employee, a gaunt, balding old timer who surveyed the world through brown, deep-set eyes gleaming from under shaggy gray brows. His name was Pike Hewson and he was one of the misfits of the territory, a taciturn, moody, friendless old bachelor, cynical in his advanced years.

After Max had introduced him to the Texans, Pike took charge of the three horses. He muttered an answer to Max's question, as he led the animals to stalls.

"It's gettin' near her time. Another hour at most."

"Sounds like I'd better hang around," frowned Max.

"With you tendin' her, she'll do fine," shrugged Pike.

He was out of earshot when Larry glanced toward the end stall and remarked,

"You got a mare about ready to foal."

"Not my mare," said Max. "She belongs to a farmer named Gaffney. He has his hands full with an over-crowded barn and, along with his other problems, his wife and younger son are laid up with influenza. So, for a small fee, I'll midwife old Clara."

"Still plenty of folks that don't call you crazy, huh?" prodded Stretch, as he squatted on a box and dug out his makings.

"I have *some* friends in the territory—just a few," shrugged Max.

"Like old Pike, for instance?" asked Larry.

52

"Strange, the way a whole community can reject a man, and only because they don't understand him," mused Max. "I know Pike's a sorehead. I know he's ugly and unsociable, but does he have to be an outcast? There should be a place for every man in every community, provided he obeys the law." Larry got the impression Max was about to enlarge on these sentiments, but the mare nickered and, with a muttered apology, Max left them for a moment. They rolled and lit cigarettes, watched him walk to the rear stall and stare in at the mare. When he rejoined them, Pike emerged from the stall where he had bedded Larry's sorrel and moved closer to listen. "We won't have to wait a whole hour," Max announced.

"I'd have sworn an hour," growled Pike. "I'll allow old Clara gets the last word, but . . ."

"Twenty minues," frowned Max.

"You mean—exactly twenty?" challenged Stretch, grinning and winking at Larry. "Not nineteen nor twenty-one? She'll start foalin' in twenty minutes?"

"What makes you so sure, Max?" asked Larry. "You see it in a dream?"

"I had a quick vision—a kind of

impression," Max confided, "just now when I looked at her."

Gruffly, old Pike assured the Texans, "If he seen it in a vision, you can bet on it. The mare will start havin' her foal in twenty minutes."

He fished out a battered watch and studied it intently.

"I'll be too busy to show you around town," said Max.

"Thanks anyway, Max," drawled Stretch. "We don't need no guide."

About to return to the end stall, Max turned to frown at the rider hustling his mount through the street entrance. Al Burchell dismounted and, as his three sidekicks moved in after him, began growling commands. The Texans were interested, but not impressed. The B-Bar boss didn't request service; he demanded it.

"Take care of our horses," he ordered Max and Pike. "Clean straw and plenty hay. No water till they've cooled down."

The other three were about to dismount, when Max rebuffed the big redhead, gently but firmly.

"Mister Burchell, I'd as soon you patronize some other stable."

Not so gentle was Pike Hewson, who curtly reminded Burchell,

"You owe for the last five times you stabled your animals here. Fitch ain't carryin' you nor more. Your credit's run out."

"Let Crazy Max talk for himself," scowled Burchell, balling his fists. "I ain't here to be back-talked by no two-bit stablehand."

"Pike saved me the trouble of saying it," muttered Max. He gestured to the entrance and began turning his back. "I'll thank you to take your animals elsewhere."

"Just a doggone minute now . . . !" began Burchell.

"And I've no time for argument," said Max. "I have to take care of a mare in foal."

"Damn you, Fitch, you're gonna make me good and mad," warned Burchell.

"Just like all the others, Al," drawled one of his cohorts. "They keep turnin' their backs on us."

"No lame-brained stableboy is gonna treat me like dirt," snarled Burchell, "just because B-Bar hit a streak of bad luck."

"It wasn't bad luck, Burchell," gibed Pike.

"*Mister* Burchell to you!" countered the redhead.

"You went broke from showin' off. Every dollar you had was wasted on cheap booze and painted whores." Pike grimaced in contempt. "Week after week, you and your no-account crew rode to Beeson's Gulch . . ."

"Shuddup, you lousy cripple!" gasped Burchell.

"And those whores were always waitin' for you," jeered Pike. "Waitin' to skin you for your last dime."

"I said *shuddup!*" raged Burchell.

He advanced on the old man, and Max reacted instinctively, sidestepping to intercept him and, as usual, not ducking fast enough. Burchell disposed of Max with a swinging back-hander that drove him four yards along the straw-littered passage. And then, as Pike warily retreated from the cursing B-Bar boss, the drifters traded glances and got to their feet.

"Would you say there's some kind of hex on little Max?" asked Stretch. "Seems every other galoot he runs into wants to beat up on him."

"Seems that way," Larry agreed.

Unhurriedly, he maneuvered himself into position, placing himself between Pike Hewson and his would-be assailant. The other B-Bar men began dismounting, but froze half-out of

56

their saddles, when Stretch drawled a command.

"Stay mounted, boys."

"Just who the hell d'you think you are?" challenged Burchell's ramrod, the shifty-eyed Jake Thornley.

"Stay mounted," Stretch repeated, "and back out."

"Jake, you keep the beanpole busy," ordered Burchell, "while I take care of his sidekick."

Max stood by the entrance to the end stall, one hand raised to his smarting face, his gaze switching from the mare to the B-Bar hard cases. Without taking his eyes off Burchell, Larry told him,

"You and Pike stay with the mare. We'll get rid of B-Bar."

"You'll do *what*?" challenged Burchell.

"You heard, Red," growled Larry. "Back out. Take your animals and your friends with you."

"Stranger, you're beggin' for it!" breathed Burchell.

And he charged right into Larry's bunched left, recoiled and backstepped to where Stretch stood. The taller Texan, with no apparent effort, spun Burchell around with the flat of his hand and kept him moving, swinging a well-aimed kick to his rear section. Yelling, Burchell hurtled past Thornley's horse and collided with the third animal, which flinched and began rearing.

There was confusion inside the barn, but only for a few moments. Mindful of the mare's condition and Max Fitch's natural anxiety, Larry and Stretch emptied the place of B-Bar men and animals in double-quick time. The startled horses were turned roughly by the Texans, who grasped their bridles and hustled them toward the entrance. When Thornely tried to swing a blow at Larry, Larry seized his boot, jerked it from the stirrup and heaved upward with all his might; Thornley joined his boss on the ground as the last horse was led out. Cursing luridly, Burchell and Thornley regained their feet and dashed out after the Texans and, from then on, events followed their natural course. The other B-Bar men swung down and aimed wild blows at Larry and Stretch, who retaliated with gusto. Burchell and Thornely tried to take them from the rear, but the Texans promptly changed position, standing back to back.

The ensuing fracas was desinted to be

discussed, described and exaggerated in the bars and barber-shops of Logantown for months to come. Logantown folk enjoyed a good ruckus, and proved it by turning out by the score. Both side-walks were crowded and, when Thornley got in the way of Stretch's flashing fist, the impact drove him into a cluster of some half-dozen locals, two of whom were knocked sprawling. Seconds later, three others were born to the dust by the bulky and off-balance Al Burchell, a victim of Larry's powerful uppercut.

As the crowd grew, the arena became over-populated. Non-combatants were forced off the sidewalks to become involved with the brawlers, and Burchell and his men were fighting wildly now; many a punch aimed at Larry or Stretch consigned an irate towner to the dust. Beside himself with rage, roaring like an injured bull, Burchell got close enough to land blows on Larry's head, but was paid off by another swinging uppercut. This time, he was sent crashing against a buggy stalled by the yelling, milling throng, and the driver gasped a reprimand and struck at him with her whip.

The B-Bar boss turned to glower at Ella Hinchley, wife of the manager of the Settlers

National. Stout and assertive, her tight-corseted frame rigged in sober bombazine, the banker's wife raised her whip again.

"Stand clear!" she ordered. "And I hope you take a beating!"

"Mother—for heaven's sake," protested her daughter.

"Stop fussing, Louise," countered Ella. "It wouldn't be the first time I've discouraged a hooligan with a buggy-whip." She lashed out at Burchell again. "Stand clear!"

"Damned old she-wolf!" snarled Burchell.

"What did he call me?" gasped Ella.

"Careful!" warned Louise. In her early 20's, the daughter of Aaron and Ella Hinchley was slender and dark-haired, but not delicate. Deftly and firmly, she relieved her mother of the reins and regained control of the startled teamers. "Hang on, Mother. I'll try to get us through to Main Street."

But the buggy moved only a few yards before stalling again. Louise had no choice but to haul back on the reins. Stretch and two of Burchell's men, entangled in a wild melee of flailing arms and threshing legs, had rolled in front of the team.

Ella Hinchley, who was inclined to be philosophical at times, shrugged helplessly, surrendered the whip to Louise and began fanning herself with a kerchief. Stuck in the middle of Colley Road, they had a clear view of the fracas and were able to identify many of the onlookers. Deputies Prowse and Dagget, stern-faced and determined, had reached the fringe of the throng and were trying to force their way through to the brawlers, but making slow going of it. Max Fitch appeared briefly in the street entrance of the Happy Haven, frowned worriedly at Larry, then glanced toward the Hinchley women. He need not have worried about Larry, who was trading blows with Thornley and getting the best of it. As his gaze locked with Louise's, Max grinned self-consciously and doffed his hat. Ella grimaced in keen disapproval.

"The dreamer again—making eyes at you."

"I'm sure he means no offense," said Louise.

"A fool who makes predictions that don't come true," gibed Ella. "He did it again today —haven't you heard? Rode out and delayed the eastbound train at Garvie's Gorge, insisted the bridge was about to fall."

"At least he was trying to help," argued Louise.

"Don't make excuses for that no-account."

"He isn't no-account, Mother. He has ambition. He'll become the county's first fully-qualified veterinarian in a few more months. He told me just the other day . . ."

"I'd as soon you had no conversation with Max Fitch," chided Ella. "It makes us nervous, your father and I, the thought of our daughter being courted by a man they call Crazy."

"That's just a cruel nickname," Louise protested.

"You're too generous for your own good," opined Ella. "It's my belief he's *earned* his nickname." She shook her head in exasperation as her gaze fastened on the scrawny, unkempt man climbing to the second floor gallery of the Peacham Hotel. "Will you look at Doc Milford —that lazy old reprobate? Drunk again. Enjoying this disgraceful spectacle, instead of trying to *do* something about it."

"I don't know if there's much Doc Milford could do," frowned Louise, "except to tend those rowdies when the fight is over." She studied the aging medico making himself comfortable on the gallery-rail and, with a soft smile, remarked, "I kind of like Doc Milford.

Maybe he *is* a reprobate, but there's something very appealing about him."

"You're becoming as muddle-brained as Max Fitch," snorted Ella.

Dr. Rufus Milford had straddled the gallery-rail and was propping his back against a porch-post. A well-gnawed cigar jutted from under his scruffy mustache. His beaver hat was slightly askew on his shaggy-thatched dome and, as usual, he was in his shirtsleeves; it had to be late fall or early winter before Logantown's laziest healer got around to wearing a coat. The vest was threadbare and one pocket bulged; Doc always toted a shot glass in there. Resting snugly in the crook of his left arm was a bottle that had once contained raw alcohol. Now, as he settled himself, dug out his glass and uncorked his bottle, Ella Hinchley shuddered. It was common knowledge that Doc Milford was addicted to his own brand of booze, some powerful concoction mixed in his surgery. Grinning contentedly, he poured himself a stiff shot, took a pull at it and added his voice to the cheers of the populace, bellowing encouragement to the brawlers.

Just as the deputies reached the combatants, Sheriff Todd Waterbury arrived and began working his way through the crowd, and his was a speedier progress; he had brought a shotgun along and was looking angry enough to use it.

"Break it up!" boomed Deputy Prowse. Aware of the two women on the buggyseat, he squared his shoulders and inflated his chest. Always the braggart, Leroy Prowse was a brawny 6-footer who liked to wear flashy range clothes and to remind the whole territory that he was a duly appointed law officer. He kept his badge well-polished, talked loudly, swaggered a lot and had become an expert at the chore of transferring drunken deadbeats from the gutters and side alleys of Main Street to the cold cells of the county jail. "Stand quiet!" he commanded, as he came up behind Larry and grasped at his arms. "That's an order, cowboy."

The second deputy hooked his bony thumbs in his bunbelt and guffawed unsympathetically, as Larry whirled quickly and slammed a fist to Prowse's jaw. Prowse loosed a startled oath and backstepped hastily, over-balancing and flopping on his backside.

"Keep it up, Leroy," leered Davey Dagget. "You're doin' just fine." Leaner than Prowse and some two inches taller, he scorned his colleague's fondness for flashy garb and wore a patched shirt and shabby denim pants that had seen better days. Prowse favored a handsome white Stetson. Dagget's headgear was a colorless, sweat-stained, floppy-brimmed wreck. Prowse visited a barber regularly. Dagget's hair hung over his collar and a four-day stubble adorned his sagging, jowly visage. "You ain't makin' much of an impresion, Leroy," he taunted, "but don't get discouraged. And remember—the ladies are still watchin'."

Larry braced himself for Burchell's last stumbling rush. Thornley was down and staying down. The third B-Bar man slumbered by the far sidewalk, nose bloody and one eye blackened, and now Stretch was disposing of the fourth, hauling him toward a hitchrail by one leg. To the great amusement of the onlookers, he draped the befuddled hard case across the rail so that he hung with legs and arms dangling. Mumbling curses, Burchell swung at Larry and missed. Larry's bunched left exploded in his face and, abruptly, he stopped cursing; his legs buckled and he flopped in an untidy heap, while Larry turned to frown at the half-prone and very indignant Leroy Prowse.

"If this galoot's a deputy, why in hell didn't he up and say so?" he challenged Dagget.

"He's supposed to say 'in the name of the law'—or somethin' like that," offered Stretch, dawdling across to join them. "We know, on account of we've heard it said before."

"Experienced, huh?" grinned Dagget.

"Well . . ." Stretch shrugged nonchalantly, "this ain't exactly the first time—you know what I mean?"

"We've been in another ruckus or three," drawled Larry.

"I'll bet," nodded Dagget, glancing at the befuddled rowdies of B-Bar.

Burchell and his men were regaining their feet, but sluggishly, when Sheriff Waterbury arrived on the scene. The crowd was dispersing, now that the excitement was over. Up on the second floor gallery of the Peacham, Doc Milford slid from his perch and ambled along to the stairs. Louise Hinchley made to drive on, but paused at Max Fitch's urgent call. He was hurrying across to the buggy, as Todd Waterbury fixed a stern but sad eye on the B-Bar men and growled a reproach.

"No use blamin' the whole town for your bad luck," he warned Burchell. "I don't have to ask

66

who started this hassle. You've been throwin' your weight around and actin' ornery ever since the bank foreclosed on your south pasture. Heed what I'm tellin' you, Burchell." He uncocked the shotgun and tucked it under an arm. "It's time you cooled your temper and got rid of that chip on your shoulder. Get off the street now—and stay out of trouble."

Battered, bruised and bitter, the four hard cases retrieved their horses, swung astride and rode slowly toward the corner of Colley and Main. The sheriff then turned his lined and white-whiskered face toward the Lone Star Hellions and, shrugging philosophically, they stood their ground and waited for the same old speech, the reprimand they had heard voiced by more lawmen than they could count on the fingers of both hands.

For a long moment, Waterbury sized them up. Then, to their astonishment, he turned his back on them and spoke to the deputies.

"Leroy—you okay?"

"These damn-blasted strangers . . . !" began Prowse. "Leroy's own blame fault," interjected Dagget.

"Leaped before he looked, huh Davey?" asked Waterbury.

"Didn't show his badge," drawled Dagget. "Just grabbed one of 'em and won hisself a faceful of knuckles."

"Damn it, I know how to break up a ruckus!" fumed Prowse. "I don't need to be told how to do my job!"

"Next time, use your badge," advised Waterbury. "Or pull your iron."

"We get paid to keep the peace, Leroy," Dagget pointed out. "Not to get clobbered by no stranger."

For Larry and Stretch, it was an intriguing and confusing moment. Time and time again, they had been marched to a cow-town poky at the point of a lawman's shotgun, after a violent hassle not of their choosing. Usually they took the blame and were accommodated at the county's expense. Here in Logantown, it was different. Old Sheriff Waterbury seemed doggedly determined *not* to arrest them; he hadn't even offered a reprimand, despite the indignation of Deputy Prowse.

While they watched, Waterbury handed his shotgun to Dagget, took a firm grip of Prowse's shoulder and began hustling him along to the intersection. Dagget sketched them a casual salute and tagged after the other lawmen, and the Texans traded wondering glances.

"Just this once," Stretch observed, "they didn't blame us."

"Mighty unusual," mused Larry.

"Plumb unnatural," declared Stretch. "Hell, runt, they *always* blame us."

"I guess there has to be a first time for everything," shrugged Larry.

At a nearby pump, they swabbed the grime and gore of battle from their faces and watched Max talking earnestly to Louise and her mother. The stalled buggy was too far away for them to eavesdrop, but they knew Max was being rebuffed; the expression on Ella Hinchley's face was eloquent.

3

"I BEG you, ma'am, to accept my advice in the spirit its offered," said Max, while the banker's wife took a firm grip of the buggy whip and eyed him balefully. "At least put the suggestion to your husband . . ."

"He *is* crazy!" Ella assured Louise. "Here it is Wednesday, and he expects us to cancel the banquet for Mister Glynn—just because he's had another dream!"

"It's a strong premonition," declared Max. "Friday will be the thirteenth . . ."

"The Hinchley family has never been superstitious!" snapped Ella.

"There'll be trouble of some kind," Max warned, "during or after the banquet. I can't predict the nature of the disaster. Maybe all the supper guests will be stricken with ptomaine or maybe the Grand Western Hotel will catch fire . . ."

"Drive on, Louise," ordered Ella. "If I have to listen to this idiot one more moment, I'll forget I'm a lady."

Pike Hewson appeared in the barn entrance, beckoning urgently.

"Mare's about ready," he called.

"I beg you to excuse me now, ladies," muttered Max, as he began retreating.

"It was kind of you to warn us, Max," murmured Louise. "I'm sure the banquet will be a big success—with no unhappy incidents—but I do thank you for your interest."

"Drive!" gasped Ella. The teamers began plodding toward the corner, Louise keeping her eyes turned toward the main stem, her mother eyeing her askance. "Since when," she demanded, "are you and that—that stablehand —on first name terms? I distinctly heard you call him 'Max'."

"He's more than a stablehand," countered Louise. "He owns . . ."

"All right, all right! I'll admit he owns that broken-down barn, but that doesn't mean he's acceptable. If he starts hanging around our home—I warn you—I'll send for the sheriff and swear out a complaint against him."

"You judge him too harshly, Mother."

"I'm taking no chances. No daughter of mine will be courted by a—a fool who has wild dreams every night of the week—who predicts

71

calamaties—who tries to scare people out of their wits . . . !"

"Max hasn't tried to court me," said Louise, as she guided the team into Main Street. "I almost wish he would."

"You'd do better to show some encouragement to that fine, upstanding Leroy Prowse," asserted Ella. "Now *he* has prospects—*real* prospects. When Todd Waterbury retires, you may be sure Leroy will become the new sheriff of Logan County."

"I'd as soon encourage Davey Dagget," retorted Louise.

"Davey Dagget is uncouth," Ella said disdainfully.

"And Leroy's a show-off," said Louise.

"I don't know what's to become of you," fretted Ella. "Twenty-two years old and still a spinster—and no gentlemen callers."

As Max reached the barn entrance, Larry called a question.

"Need any help?"

"I can manage," said Max.

"All right, boy, stay with it," nodded Larry. "We'll find us a hotel and get back to you later."

Toting their saddlebags, packrolls and rifles,

the Texans sauntered along to Main Street and began their brief search for accommodation. In the barn, Max knelt beside the mare, patted her mane and muttered a comforting word, and nature took over; the process of birth began.

"Twenty minutes," Pike quietly announced, squinting at his watch. "Twenty minutes exactly."

Two blocks uptown, Al Burchell and his men emerged from yet another livery stable, the third they had visited since the hullabaloo on Colley Road. The merchants, saloonkeepers and stablehands of Logantown had tired of B-Bar's bullying tactics; well aware that Burchell and his men were short of cash, they refused to be intimidated. The stablehand at the Rest-Up Livery had done his talking from behind a levelled shotgun.

"We all let you push us around before, Burchell, but only because you paid your bills," he had told the rancher. "Now it's different. You ain't askin' for credit—you're demandin' it—and we've taken all the pushin' we're gonna take. Pay cash, or use some other barn."

In a black mood, Burchell led his men another half-block uptown. They tethered their mounts outside a small bar, the Lucky Seven, and the B-Bar boss curtly announced.

"We'll buy a bottle, have us a few drinks and head on back to the ranch. What the hell *else* can we do?"

"Can't afford to play the tables at Crane's place, and *that's* for sure," growled Thornley. "It takes mucho dinero—more than we got."

They tramped into the barroom and, at once, Burchell was conscious of the derisive grins of the other customers, townmen who had seen B-Bar—a 4-man outfit—battered and beaten by a couple of hard-hitting drifters.

"Wipe that grin off of your face and put up a pint of rye," he sourly ordered the barkeep.

"Cash first, Burchell," countered the barkeep. "Boss's orders."

Burchell cursed bitterly, dropped cash on the bar and watched the barkeep make change, then snatched the bottle and demanded four glasses.

"We'll do our drinkin' private," he told his men, as he made for a rear door.

In one of the small rooms used for private poker parties, the four hard cases swigged rye, smoked cheap cigars and discussed their futures.

"Only one way you can make the old spread

74

pay off," the ramrod warned Burchell. "You'd need two good seasons to get back on your feet, and every dime you can raise would have to be spent on breed-stock. That means we'd have to live quiet, Al."

"A man might's well be dead," complained the third hard case, "Unless we got cash in our pockets—and plenty of it—them women at the Gulch are gonna close their doors against us." Cardew was his name and, ironically, he fancied himself as a womaniser; he was the ugliest of the four. His broad, unshaven visage creased in a scowl of disgust as he repeated, "A man might's well be dead."

"There's sucker gamblers at the Gulch," muttered the fourth man, Hale. He held a wet bandana to a badly bruised eye, but, already, he was forgetting the Texans. Poker was his passion, and he liked to make his own luck. His colt was worn at his left hip with the butt jutting forward for a crossdraw. "Give me just two days at the old Beeson's Gulch Casino," he breathed. "All I need is a couple hundred dollars—and then I'd show you some fast and fancy poker. I'd teach those tinhorns a lesson they'd never forget."

"So you need cash, Hale," shrugged

Thornley. "That means you ain't no different from the rest of us."

"Hinchley . . ." Burchell mouthed the name grimly. "Aaron Hinchley and his high falutin' womenfolk and his tin can bank—his strongroom—all that beautiful cash . . ."

"Take it easy, Al," chided Thornley. "Leave all the wild dreamin' to Crazy Max."

"It'd pleasure me, and that's a fact," declared Burchell. "I crave to see him on his knees, to hear him whine. And the whole town laughin' at him—him that claims the Settlers National can't ever be robbed."

"That's somethin' to brag about," shrugged Hale. "He's been in the business better than twenty years and never lost a dime of the bank's money. Quite a record."

"I'd enjoy to bust his almighty record," Burchell said savagely. "Never was a bank that couldn't be robbed. What's so special about the Settlers National? Tell me *that*."

"I guess it's just never been tried," said Hale.

"Well, by Judas, *I'm* ready to try," asserted Burchell.

"You mean that?" challenged Thornley.

"Damn right I mean it," growled Burchell. "And I'll tell you when I'd do it. I'd do it

76

Friday night—while Hinchley and his big boss are eatin' fancy chow and drinkin' champagne at the Grand Western—while this feller Glynn is pattin' Hinchley's back and makin' him a speech and all." He chuckled harshly. "There couldn't be a better time."

"Hinchley'd look mighty foolish," frowned Cardew.

"I owe him—damn his soul," breathed Burchell. "I owe him for when he foreclosed on my whole south pasture—and then sold it to Rafter J—the land, the graze, the water that used to be all mine . . ."

"You put up them acres as security against a loan," Thornley reminded him. "Hinchley gave you time to pay . . ."

"Whose side are you on?" snapped Burchell.

"No need to get sore, Al," shrugged Thornley. "I don't admire Hinchley any more than you do. If you want to bust the Settlers National and get rich in a hurry, that's just fine by me. Only . . ."

"Only what?"

"Only I don't savvy how you could do it."

Burchell thought about it a moment. Thornley eyed him warily, while Cardew and Hale refilled their glasses and swapped frowns.

And then, bluntly, Burchell declared, "We can do it—and get away with it—if we work fast. Best way in would be the rear door. We force it. One man stands by and keeps an eye on the alley, and our horses."

"Sounds okay—so far," drawled Cardew. "But what about that vault door?"

"We blast it open," said Burchell.

"You mean . . . ?" began Thornley.

"I mean we got one bundle left, just one bundle and enough fuse," said Burchell. "Remember when I tried to start a new water-hole in the south quarter last summer? We dug us a hole, planted dynamite with a long fuse . . ."

"Blew up a mess of dirt and rock," recalled Hale, "but no water."

"Al, they'll hear the blast all over town," warned Thornley.

"I still say we can get away with it," insisted Burchell. "But it has to be handled fast and slick. We fill a sack with greenbacks and get out of there muy pronto. By the time Water-bury and his deputies show, we could be out of the rear alley and ridin' north along the old McGowan road."

"That's a helluva trail for a getaway," argued Cardew.

"Ain't been travelled in years," frowned Hale. "Brush growin' half-way across it."

"So we ride in Indian file," said Burchell, "all the way to Snyder Rock, while Waterbury's posse travels the regular stage route."

"From the Rock, we could reach home range in a quarter-hour," mused Thornley. "Maybe Al's notion ain't so wild after all. Last place they'd think of findin' us is along the old McGowan road."

"Friday night, huh?" prodded Cardew.

"Any arguments?" challenged Burchell.

"No arguments," shrugged Cardew. "But I got a question. Do we quit the territory, or do we hang around a while?"

"We daren't run out the same night the bank is robbed," opined Thornley.

"He was askin' *me*," chided Burchell. Then, to Cardew and Hale, he admitted, "What Jake says is right anyway. If we quit the county Friday night, Waterbury'd do some fast guessin'. Then he'd telegraph all the other badge-toters hereabouts and, no matter which way we travelled, there'd be some posses huntin' us."

79

"So we sit on the loot maybe a couple weeks, huh Al?" Thornley suggested.

"A couple weeks," nodded Burchell. "Just long enough for the whoopin' and hollerin' to die down. And then we'll be on our way." He grinned derisively at Cardew. "Maybe Beeson's Gulch is good enough for you. Me, I'll be headed a damn sight farther than the Gulch. Straight to Cheyenne and south into Colorado. I hear Denver's got plenty of everything."

"We ought to talk it over some more," said Thornley. "Like you said, Al, it has to be fast and slick. So we got to plan every move we make."

"Cork that bottle," Burchell ordered Hale, as he got to his feet. "We're movin' out now."

He had almost reached the doorway and his men were rising to follow him, when the door opened. The man on the threshold grinning a challenge at the B-Bar men was known to Logantown as Sam Parrant, attorney at law, sucker gambler, compulsive drinker and an opportunist to his well-manicured fingertips. A Long 9 drooped from the thick-lipped mouth. The nose was too small for the moon face and a beard would have been an improvement, possibly camouflaging the receding chin. Parrant was flabby and indolent, a lawyer who had seen better days; his practice barely paid his room rent. The striped pants, black Prince Albert and white linen were of fine quality, but grubby. He winked at Burchell, puffed at his cigar and muttered a suggestion.

"Talk it over again by all means. Plan every move carefully."

"He heard!" gasped Thornley.

"Shuddup!" snarled Burchell.

"The walls are thin, Burchell." Parrant propped a shoulder against the door jamb. His grin broadened. He was poised, at his ease and very sure of himself. When Burchell began advancing on him, he raised a hand languidly. "Careful, my friend. Let's not get physical. There are too many witnesses." Burchell came to an abrupt halt. "That's better. We'll talk quietly and calmly now."

"Lousy snooper," breathed Thornley.

"Couldn't help overhearing," shrugged Parrant. "Fortunately I was alone. I like privacy when I play solitaire."

"In the next room?" challenged Hale, glancing to the wall at his left.

"And not snooping, Thornley," said Parrant, grinning at the ramrod.

81

"Just listenin'," accused Thornley.

"With keen interest," Parrant assured him. He looked at Burchell again. "I won't delay you, Burchell. You'll be wanting to get back to B-Bar and make your plans. Go right ahead. But, when you're tallying the proceeds of your enterprise, don't forget me."

"And what's that supposed to mean?" demanded Burchell.

"Burchell, that's a mighty foolish question— and unnecessary," drawled Parrant. "You *know* what it means."

"He's dealin' himself in," scowled Cardew.

"For a half share," nodded Parrant.

"For—*what* . . . ?" began Burchell.

"Fifty percent," Parrant said firmly. "Whatever you take from the vault at the Settlers National, we split it right down the middle. I'm taking half, Burchell. And, before you start bellowing—inviting the attention of the barkeep and his customers—I suggest you consider the alternative. If I went to Todd Waterbury right now and repeated what I'd heard . . ."

"All right." Burchell sighed heavily and bowed his head. "All right, lawyer-man. You made your point."

"I'll ride out to B-Bar Friday night," said

82

Parrant. "When you arrive, I'll be glad to help tally the loot." He chuckled softly. "I doubt if you've counted so much cash before, Burchell, and we wouldn't want you to make any errors, would we? When I say fifty percent, I mean *exactly* fifty percent."

"Heard you the first time, lawyer-man," muttered Burchell.

He brushed past the grinning attorney and, tagged by his men, trudged across the barroom and out into the street. Thornley stood beside him as he slipped his rein.

"Hell, Al, he heard everything! And, no matter how much dinero we grab from that vault, we've lost half already!"

"We ain't lost a dime, Jake," countered Burchell. He glared over his shoulder, dropped his voice to a husky whisper and assured the ramrod, "Parrant just now signed his own death warrant."

By sundown, Larry and Stretch had checked into the Heenan Hotel, a cheap rooming house in the heart of town. It was small and poky, but the Lone Star Hellions weren't seeking luxury accommodation. They disposed of a substantial supper at a downtown restaurant, then stopped by the Happy Haven to invite Max to join them and to check on the mare.

"A colt," Max announced, as they ambled into the barn. "Handsome little feller too. Come take a look."

He puffed at a straight-stemmed brier and gestured for them to inspect the occupants of the end stall. Pike Hewson squatted on a stool at the rear of the passage, swigging coffee and contentedly inspecting the new arrival. For a fleeting moment, the sensitive-faced amateur vet and his aged helper put Larry in mind of a new father and grandfather. Stretch tagged him to the end stall. They studied the mare and her foal a moment, nodded howdy to Pike, then extended their invitation. Would Max care to celebrate the colt's arrival and join them for a few drinks?

"I'm not much of a drinking man," Max confided, as he donned his hat, "but I'll be glad to join you."

"Had your supper?" asked Larry.

"Oh, sure," nodded Max. "An hour ago. The mare gave us no trouble at all, and she's been resting easily ever since."

"We been thinkin', Max boy," drawled Stretch, "about what you said today . . ."

"I've probably said a great deal today."

"You know what I mean. About how Larry ought to play the roulette layout at the Wheel Of Fortune."

"Oh. That?"

"Yeah. That."

"Well, I did get a strong impression," Max recalled. "Brief, but strong. Larry winning at Phil Crane's wheel . . ."

"Playin' the even numbers, you said," Stretch reminded him.

"You'd risk hard cash—just on my hunches?" Max challenged Larry. "Surely you don't believe in my intuition, my second sight? Few people do, Larry, so why should you be any exception?"

"Let's just say I'm curious," grinned Larry, taking his arm.

At 7 p.m., when the Texans entered the Wheel Of Fortune with Max Fitch in tow, they won little attention from Phil Crane's barkeeps and tablemen. The gaudily-gowned percenters looked them over and, noting their shabby attire, decided to wait for richer pickings. They made for the roulette table, watched with only casual interest by the saloonkeeper, who occupied his usual table and quietly conversed with Rose Dawes.

"I'm a man of my word," he calmly assured the blonde woman. "You're bait for Taflin, sweetheart, and that's as far as you go with him. You can turn your back on him as soon as we've collected our share. He'll be a sore loser, but he daren't make trouble for us. He can't run to the law, can't turn us in without putting himself behind bars."

"Just so long as we understand one another, Phil," she warned. "When it's over, when you sell the Wheel Of Fortune and quit the territory, you won't be travelling alone."

"Wouldn't want to," he smiled, placing a hand on hers. "By then, my dear, you'll be Mrs. Phil Crane, and we'll travel in style."

Twenty minutes later, a few moments before Jay Taflin arrived, Crane was again glancing to the roulette layout, but not casually; he had sensed the change in the atmosphere, the increasing excitement of the locals milling about the table, some of them to encourage the Texans, some to bid for a piece of the action. The croupier's face was shiny with sweat; he looked harassed.

"Go check the roulette set-up," he ordered

Rose. "I don't like that worried look on Marty's face."

The croupier mumbled his invitation and frowned uncertainly at the tall strangers.

"Place your bets, gents. Wheel's about to spin again." He saw Max nudge Larry and point to a numbered square. "Listen—just what's the big idea here? You jaspers got some kind of system?"

"Just playin' hunches, amigo," grinned Stretch.

"The whole bundle?" Larry asked Max.

"You might as well," shrugged Max. "The impression was very clear. I don't see how you could lose."

As Larry dropped a wad of bills on the red square numbered 8, the croupier squinted incredulously.

"*That* much?" he challenged. "You sure you know what you're doing?"

"Haven't missed yet, have I?" countered Larry.

"This is plain crazy," mumbled the croupier, mopping his brow.

"Amigo, you dunno how true that is," chuckled Stretch.

"Place your bets, gents . . ." The croupier

waited a few more moments, then started his wheel spinning. Wide-eyed and expectant, the locals leaned closer, listening to the cheerful clatter of the tiny white ball, watching it dance and jiggle from hollow to hollow and then, when the wheel slowed, settle firmly into hole Number 8. Starting convulsively, gaping at the Texans, the croupier complained, "It's not *natural!*"

"Quit your belly-achin' and pay up," growled Larry, while Stretch grinned cheerfully at their audience. "There's no way a player can cheat at this game."

"My friend was betting on a certainty," Max calmly informed the croupier.

"You been having visions again, Fitch?" asked the croupier.

"It happens all the time," said Max. "Larry, have you had enough?" He yawned and stared wistfully toward the batwings. "I didn't get much sleep last night. Maybe tonight there'll be no bad dreams."

"I reckon we've had enough, huh runt?" drawled Stretch.

"Why, sure," agreed Larry. "Hey, you with the nervous eyes, how much have we won?"

"In thirty minutes, you won on eight turns

of the wheel," muttered the croupier, as he delved into his cashbox. "I call it downright unnatural . . ." he made a few calculations, shrugged helplessly and offered Larry his winnings. "Here it is. Close enough to three thousand."

"Yow-eee!" whooped Stretch. "This here's our night to howl!"

"Max, part of this is rightly yours," declared Larry, as he stowed the thick wad in his hip pocket.

"You owe me nothing," said Max, yawning again. "Anyway—do you mind if we argue about it tomorrow? I can barely keep my eyes open."

"Okay, Maxie boy," grinned Stretch. "We buy you one for the road and then we tell you buenas noches."

They hustled the dreamer across to the bar and ordered double shots of the best bourbon, while Rose Dawes returned to Phil Crane's private table to report,

"Marty dropped almost three thousand to those Texas saddletramps."

"Three thousand?" Crane swore softly. "Three thousand—at roulette—in less than a half-hour?"

"The way Marty tells it, they just couldn't go wrong," she shrugged. "Crazy Max told 'em where to place their bets—and they won every time."

"That's downright unnatural!"

"That's what Marty says, But it happened."

Covertly, Crane studied the three men at the bar; Max was stifling his yawns long enough to dispose of a shot of bourbon, while the Texans grinned amiably and patted his back.

"They're roughnecks," he quietly opined. "Big money is wasted on the likes of them."

"Three thousand is chicken-feed," Rose pointed out, "compared with your share of . . ."

"Send Jerry to me," muttered Crane.

"And Jerry'll pass the word to Rafe and Steve," she guessed, smiling scornfully. "Your three plug—uglies will tag those winners, beat them senseless in some back alley and get back your three thousand. Is it all that important to you, Phil?"

"You might say it's a matter of principle," drawled Crane.

"It could be a mighty foolish mistake," she warned. "Didn't you hear about the ruckus on Colley Road? Al Burchell and his crew had a run-in with the Texans—and lost. Four against two, and the two were still on their feet when the law arrived to break it up."

"Burchell and his men are no-accounts," shrugged Crane "Jerry and Rafe and Steve— they're experts. Fitch's roughneck friends won't know what hit 'em."

"I'll fetch Jerry," she frowned. "But—I hope you know what you're doing."

A short time later, when the Texans walked Max out of the Wheel Of Fortune, they were followed at a respectful distance by three of Crane's employees; a burly barkeep, a faro-dealer and the bouncer. Reaching the corner of Main and Colley, Max bade the drifters good-night and headed for home. The Texans paused under a street-lamp to rool and light cigarettes, while Crane's hirelings watched from a dark doorway some 30 yards away.

"The night's still young," Larry remarked. "What d'you say we try some other saloon, maybe find us a high stake poker party?"

"Let's not get greedy." Stretch was inclined to be cautious, thinking of their winnings. "That's more dinero than we've had in many a long year. So lets head on back to our room and talk about it." He yawned and stretched.

"Doggone little Max. Watchin' him yawn has made me tired."

When the Texans moved off again, the barkeep, the faro-dealer and the bouncer began shadowing them. It was a slow progress, because Larry and Stretch were taking their time; they had no reason to hustle. And, for a full block, they walked the well-lit areas, so that Jerry, Rafe and Steve were obliged to postpone their attack.

The Heenan Hotel was located on Logan Street, which ran parallel with Main and could be reached by any one of a number of connecting alleys. When the Texans turned into one of those alleys, the three hard cases saw their opportunity—or thought they did. Unfortunately they were ignorant of the fact that Deputies Prowse and Dagget had entered that alley a few moments before, taking a short-cut to Logan Street as part of their regular nightly patrol.

The deputies were half-way along the alley and moving slowly, when Larry and Stretch reached the alleymouth. And then, a few seconds after they had disappeared from view of the men stalking them, they heard their names called. Dr. Rufus Milford's surgery had a side window opening onto the alley. He was perched on the window-ledge, drawling a greeting and an invitation. In one hand he held a half-smoked cigar, in the other a bottle that won the Texans' immediate interest.

"Mister Valentine and Mr. Emerson—better known as the Texas Hell-Raisers." Doc grinned knowingly, tucked the bottle under an arm and crooked a finger. "Come visit with me a while. We'll talk of Logantown and cattle-town medicine and good booze—and dreamers who make predictions that sometimes come true."

"Runt, how could we pass up such an invite?" challenged Stretch.

"Wouldn't want to hurt the doc's feelin's, would we?" grinned Larry. "Doc, you got yourself a couple guests."

"We won't stand on ceremony," said Doc. "If you go around front and ring the bell, I'll have to expend precious energy traipsing along the hall to admit you. If you'll climb through this window, we'll get to our drinking and socializing that much faster."

The drifters climbed through Doc Milford's surgery window. Doc lowered the shade exactly two seconds before Crane's men entered the alley from Main Street and sighted the two dimly-visible figures moving toward the Logan Street end.

"We couldn't pick a better place," opined the bouncer. "Right here in the alley—where it's dark."

"What're we waitin' for?" challenged the faro-dealer.

In the cluttered and untidy surgery, Doc motioned for his guests to take their ease. Larry chose the chair beside the wash-basin. Stretch settled for the table at which Doc examined his patients, and followed the medico's movements with an approving eye; Doc had unearthed a couple of extra glasses and was pouring from his bottle.

"This is gonna impress you," he assured them. "I don't claim you'll enjoy it. You might even be inclined to criticize it. But one thing I guarantee. You'll be impressed. You just can't ignore the effect of my private stock."

"Private stock?" prodded Stretch. "You get it shipped in special, Doc?"

"Hell, no," grinned Doc. "It's my own special blend—prepared right here in my surgery."

"Sounds interesting," remarked Larry.

"Interesting—the right word." Doc nodded

approvingly. "Yes indeed, my hard-fisted friends, it can truthfully be claimed that no drinking man worthy of the name could be bored by Milford's Boosted Bourbon thats my pet name for it. Like it? Milford's Boosted Bourbon?"

Larry took a sip, then a mouthful, savored the taste a moment, then swallowed it. The fiery liquor struck his innards aggressively. His eyes watered, but he was born game. He downed another mouthful and showed Doc a companionable grin. Simultaneously, Stretch sampled his share, shuddered and loosed an oath, but followed the oath with a satisfied chuckle.

"Good?" asked Doc.

"Good," said Larry, "is puttin' it mild."

"This here's the best damn booze I've tasted since I can't remember when," declared Stretch.

"In comparison," bragged Doc, "the watery rye sold in the saloons of Logantown pales into insignificance." He paused, cocking an ear. "You boys hear that?"

"Sounds like a ruckus," drawled Larry.

"Well, what do we care?" shrugged Stretch.

"Let it happen—and let's you and me pretend like we never heard nothin'."

"I'll drink to that," said Larry.

"Not by yourself you won't," said Stretch, lifting his glass again.

"It *is* a ruckus," said Doc. He set his glass down, returned to the window and raised the shade. Thrusting his head out, staring toward the Logan Street end of the alley, he reported the proceedings. "Looks like they're hitting each other with everything—including pistols. I'd say there's three of 'em at least—though it's hard to tell. They're in a tangle. No, wait. More than three of 'em. I'd say five."

"Who's winnin'?" asked Stretch, his tone suggesting he didn't care a damn.

"I can't see who's fighting," shrugged Doc, "so it doesn't much matter who's winning. This damn alley is poorly lit. I'll have to complain to Mayor Ashworth and his hard-bellied aldermen friends. Here we have five healthy citizens staging a slugging match, and their efforts are *wasted*. No audience."

The ruckus came to an abrupt conclusion. Doc heard a couple of thuds followed by a stream of curses and a snapping, clinking sound. A few moments later, the barkeep and bouncer from the Wheel Of Fortune came trudging toward him, their hands manacled behind their backs, their faces battered and bloody. Just as battered were Deputies Prowse and Dagget, but they had the satisfaction of having won the fight. The faro-dealer was beyond feeling pain. Unconscious, he hung over Prowse's shoulders.

"Keep movin', you sneakin', lousy side-winders," growled Dagget, his cocked .45 at the bouncer's back. "We got a cell at the cala-boose just about your size, Jarry Hyne."

"The nerve of these galoots!" raged Prowse. "The stone-cold *nerve* . . . !"

"Greetings, defenders of the peace," called Doc. "Is that you, Leroy Prowse? Uh huh. I thought as much. Well, this is a change from bullying kids for spitting on the sidewalks and helping old ladies across the street. Good to see you earning what the county pays you, Prowse."

"How'd you like to go leap in the river?" snarled Prowse. "You damn whisky-swillin' old butcher . . . !"

"Temper, temper," chided Doc. "Let's have some respect for the medical profession."

"Doc, you been feedin' any of that fire-water

to Phil Crane's hired help?" asked Davey Dagget, pausing a moment.

"That's who they are?" prodded Doc. He surveyed Dagget's prisoners casually. "No, I don't entertain saloon-workers. The way I see it, they get all the booze they need from their boss. Hey, Davey, may I ask a fair question? Why in blazes did Crane's men attack you?"

"Beats me," shrugged Dagget.

"Well . . ." Doc grinned insolently at the bruised and irate Leroy Prowse and remarked to Dagget, "I guess they don't like the company you keep."

"Nobody likes a smart-mouthed sawbones," snapped Prowse.

"Nor a bone-headed deputy," jeered Doc, "with an exaggerated notion of his own importance."

"C'mon, Leroy," urged Dagget. "Best get these galoots stashed in cells."

The lawmen and their prisoners moved on. Doc rejoined his guests, dismissing the fracas as unworthy of their attention.

"Just a minor skirmish between the law and the lawless," he shrugged, flopping into his chair. "I may include a paragraph on Davey Dagget in my chronicle of Logantown, along

with a one-age tribute to the estimable Sheriff
Waterbury. But Leroy Prowse doesn't rate a
mention. He's a blow-hard, and heaven help
Logan County if he ever gets to be sheriff."
Noting their bemused expressions, he calmly
explained, "I amuse myself by compiling a
history of this town and its more important citizens. Who knows? At some time in the dim and
distant future—long after I'm dead and gone
—some whimsical publisher may circulate my
memoirs for the whole world to read. Or at least
these United States."

"Beats me how you'd find time for all that
writin'," said Larry, as Doc exhibited his 3-inch
thick manuscript. "Every cowtown sawbones I
ever knew, why, he was kept so busy he scarce
had time to scratch himself."

"You're speaking of the *old* Rufus Milford,"
chuckled Doc. "Ah, yes, I kept busy in the
old days. Always the idealist—dedicated to the
service of my fellow-man. Used to struggle from
my lonely bachelor cot in the dead of a winter's
night to deliver babies and set broken bones
and patch bullet wounds. When they needed
good Doc Milford, he was always there."

"And then?" prodded Larry.

"The population increased," frowned Doc,

taking a stiff pull at his drink. "Some men prospered. I should have, but didn't, because too many of my patients were tight-fisted. Let me clarify that. When I know a patient is too broke to pay for my services, I don't even send a bill. It was the pikers who kept me poor. You'd be surprised how many well-heeled store-keepers and cattlemen owe me for medical attention." He snorted in disgust. "Tightwads. Skinflints. The hell with 'em all. I became a cynic." Beaming happily, he gestured for them to hold their glasses closer; his hand was steady as he poured refills. "Confidentially, my friends, I've been a damn sight happier since I became a cynic. The idealist has to stay on the move and be fast on his feet—poor, dumb bastard. The cynic—lucky sonofagun—can afford to be lazy."

"How about your patients?" asked Larry, trading grins with Stretch.

"*What* patients?" challenged Doc. "Now-adays, Logantown has three resident phys-icians—if you want to include me. One of my new colleagues is the youthful and conscientious Doctor Hyram Allgood, a mere boy aged thirty-two or thereabouts. Full of zeal is young Hyram." He raised his glass. "Gentlemen, I give you a toast. To my much respected colleagues, Hyram Allgood and Fred Torrance. May they enjoy good health and the strength to attend and succor the sick and the needy—so that Doc Milford may pursue his pastimes without interruption."

"We'll drink to that," said Larry.

And they drank and talked with the raffish healer, while a towner hurried into the Wheel Of Fortune to report that the barkeep, the bouncer and the faro-dealer had been arrested and thrown into jail for trying to beat up Deputies Prowse and Dagget. At the time of this announcement, Phil Crane was playing host to Morrison, Kilburn and Taflin at his private table. For their benefit he tried to maintain his calm, but failed. A lurid oath erupted from him.

"Those damn fools! Why in thunderation did they attack Waterbury's deputies?" He mumbled an apology and got to his feet. "I'll get back to you later. I'm short-handed now. With the bouncer, one barkeep and a tableman in jail, I'll have to lend a hand."

In his cabin across the alley from the Happy Haven barn, Max Fitch had been asleep almost a half-hour, and now the vision was returning.

Vague at first, it became clearer, so clear the dream seemed real. His pillow and mattress became damp with sweat. He tossed and turned and groaned and the scene was still sharply etched; he couldn't shut it out. Garvie's Gorge as viewed from the east side. The bridge extending from edge to edge, but no longer straight. It sagged drunkenly and, high and shrill, like a soul in torment, he heard the whistle of the eastbound train . . .

He came wide awake, panting heavily, his eyes wild.

"They won't believe me—but they *must*. I have to reach them, warn them make them understand. If they won't listen to me, there's only one other way. I have to convince somebody they *will* listen to—somebody important."

Quickly and too rashly, he made his decision, struggling from his bed and dressing in frantic haste, then dashing out into the night.

It didn't occur to Max to go talk to the sheriff or to a doctor. His destination was a handsome, double-storied home in Logantown's best residential section, the home of Aaron Hinchley.

4

"I'M a man of many parts, now that I have the time to indulge myself," Doc Milford informed his guests. In the poky surgery, the atmosphere was pungent but friendly, the odor of tobacco smoke mingling with the varied smells of raw spirits, whiskey, carbolic and iodine. "The trunk in my bedroom is filled with keepsakes, momentos souvenired from famous identities who have passed through Logantown from time to time."

"I bet Doc owns one of Bill Hickok's fancy shirts," grinned Stretch.

"No," said Doc. "But I could show you a lock of his hair, and a jack-knife used by John Wesley Hardin to notch a six-shooter. Also I own a paper collar once worn by Buffalo Bill Cody and a bible said to have been carried by the notorios Roy Bean while he was leading his guerilla band in New Mexico." He toasted his guests again, took a swig of his surgery blended whiskey and eyed them expectantly, "What

103

kind of souvenir will *you* leave in Logantown to be stored in my trunk?"

"Hell, Doc, we ain't special," shrugged Stretch. "Just a couple peace-lovin' Texans passin' through."

"You think I don't have ears to hear with, eyes to see with?" challenged Doc. "Think I can't read a newspaper or remember a face in a photograph? I recognized you two while you were whuppin' the tar out of Al Burchell and his no-account crew." Grinning smugly, he recalled, "I told 'em years ago, when Logantown started getting bigger, told Mayor Ashworth and his aldermen. "All trails will lead to and through Logantown," I said. "Sooner or later, we'll see 'em right there on Main Street and in the saloons. The famous and the infamous." Cody and Hickok came and went their way. Doc Holliday stopped by. I remember him well. He shoved a pistol in my face when I offered to prescribe for his cough. Didn't realize rightaway that he was consumptive. Bat Masterson passed through a couple of years back—now *there's* a jaunty character. He and Davey Dagget had a little private shooting contest. For targets they used high cards stuck to the top of the fence behind the old Bailey barn. I could show you an ace of clubs drilled dead center by a slug from the custom-made Colt of Mister William Barclay Masterson."

"Who else came by?" asked Stretch.

"Don't change the subject," chided Doc. "What kind of a souvenir will I get from the Lone Star Hellions?"

"We'll think of somethin'." Stretch promised.

"Doc, seein' as how you know every Logan County citizen . . ." began Larry.

"They'll all get a mention in my chronicle of the territory," declared Doc, patting his manuscript. "You curious about any particular citizen, Larry? All you have to do is ask. Name me a name, and I'll tell you *anything*." he amended that rash offer. "Well—I'll tell you as much as I think you ought to know."

"For a starter, how about Max?" challenged Larry. "We don't believe he's crazy . . ."

"You're observant, as well as charitable," shrugged Doc. "He's as sane as any of us. To study veterinary science by correspondence, operating a livery stable for the sake of practical experience, demands at least an average intelligence. Young Max is nobody's fool."

"But?" prodded Larry.

"Unfortunately Max can give the *impression* of madness," frowned Doc. "He becomes uncommonly agitated when people refuse to heed his warnings. And—I want to be fair about this—Max isn't always right. Far from it. He's predicted many a catastrophe that never occurred."

"Tonight, at the Wheel Of Fortune, we won us a bundle," countered Larry. "Roulette."

"Fortunate is the man who can win at roulette," Doc remarked.

"We dropped our dinero where Max said drop it," said Larry.

"And he was right every time," drawled Stretch. "*Every* time."

"A happy talent," Doc commented.

"You think it was accidental?" asked Larry.

"We can use that kind of accident," chuckled Stretch.

"Who couldn't?" Doc grinned and nodded. "And it's not the first time he's been right. But, as I said before . . ." He shrugged helplessly, "he's been too often wrong."

"So folks call him crazy," mused Stretch. "They remember when he was wrong, but forget when he was right."

"That's life, my friends," said Doc. "Max

Fitch is what I'd call a prophet without honor in his own community." He lit another cigar and confided, "I observe and I record. By Godfrey, if my chronicle were published tomorrow, there'd be some red faces in Logan County. Oh, well. Home truths are never appreciated. I could hardly expect Leroy Prowse to enjoy being called a self-opinionated jackass, nor would Phil Crane take kindly to my assessment of his character. A conniver, that one. Potentially treacherous, unless I miss my guess."

"Hey, Doc," grinned Stretch, "don't you know nothin' good about nobody?"

"Why, certainly," said Doc. "Logantown has many admirable identities. Our sheriff, for instance, is a rough diamond with plenty of integrity. Davey Dagget is the roughest diamond of all. I'd trust him with my life. And Louise, daughter of banker Hinchley and the apple of Max's eye—what a deceptive character . . ."

"You mean Max took a shine to a sneaky female?" asked Stretch.

"Don't misunderstand," said Doc. "Louise isn't deliberately deceptive. It's quite unintentional. All I mean is she's considerably shrewder than she appears to be. . . . What's more, she has a sense of humor."

The medico poured more refills and talked on, happy to have an attentive and congenial audience. And Larry, keenly interested in Doc's description of the local scene, spared no thought for Max Fitch, taking it for granted Max was safe in bed.

By now, Max had reached the Hinchley home, only to find that the family had retired; the place was in darkness.

"So I have to disturb him," he reflected, as he pounded on the front door. "Better to interrupt Mister Hinchley's sleep than to pretend I don't *know*. I saw what I saw, and now . . ." He pounded lounder, "I just have to make him understand."

Three minutes later, the Hinchleys and their housemaid were wide awake and in a state of confusion. The maid had unlocked and opened the door; Max had marched resolutely into the hall and insisted on talking to the banker, who came hustling downstairs with his nightshirt flapping and his snowy hair tousled. Close behind Hinchley came his formidable spouse. Louise, less excitable than her parents, advanced no further than the top of the stairs.

From there, she nodded politely to Max, who finally got around to doffing his hat and explaining himself.

"I had a dream tonight—a dream I've had before," he told the banker. "Please believe me, Mister Hinchley. The bridge at Garvie's Gorge —it just isn't safe. It could collapse any time from now on . . ."

"This is the most ridiculous thing I ever heard of!" gasped Hinchley. "Young man, if this is your idea of a joke . . . !"

"Waking us at this hour!" fumed Ella. "He must be out of his mind! He *is* out of his mind!"

"I assure you, ma'am, I'm in full possession of my faculties," declared Max. "Mister Hinchley, I urge you—I beg you—to wire the headquarters of the Trans-West Railroad. Tell them to re-route all east and westbound trains, to bypass Garvie's Gorge . . ."

"*You* telegraphed the railroad authorities," Hinchley grimly reminded him. "Two weeks ago you caused a twelve-hour delay in their schedule. It took them that long to dispatch an engineer to the gorge to check every section of the bridge—and he found no defects—nothing to indicate the bridge might fall."

109

"They won't listen to me . . ." fretted Max.

"I should hope not," growled Hinchley.

"But they'd have to heed *you*," insisted Max. "As one of our most important citizens . . ."

"Flattery will get you nowhere, young feller."

"You have a great responsibility in this matter, Mister Hinchley. Would you want the death of Mister Casper Glynn on your conscience? Isn't he scheduled to travel here on Friday's eastbound?"

Hinchley turned red, as he asked,

"Are you suggesting I should wire Mister Glynn to cancel his trip—because you've been dreaming again?"

"His is not the only life at stake," asserted Max.

"Out!" gasped the banker, pointing to the front door. "Get out and stay out! You've pestered Todd Waterbury with this crazy story. You woke Mayor Ashworth in the middle of the night and now you're plaguing me! Confound you, Fitch, do you intend working your way through every house in town?"

"The railroad engineer must have overlooked something, some important detail," argued

110

Max. "Believe me, Mister Hinchley, that bridge is a death-trap."

"*Out!*" said Hinchley.

"I'm sorry." Max moved across to the stairs and seated himself. "I refuse to budge until I'm given a hearing. The situation is desperate, so I must resort to desperate measures."

"Hannah—go find the sheriff!" ordered Ella.

As the housemaid hurried away, Louise called a reproach.

"Mother—really—do you have to go *that* far?"

"He gives us no choice," complained Ella. "If he's not removed by force, he'll still be here in the morning—and that's a mighty unpleasant prospect!"

By midnight, when Larry and Stretch finally parted company with the talkative Doc Milford, Max Fitch was well and truly installed in the county jail. Transferring him to the calaboose had become a somewhat involved operation, beginning with the sheriff's entering the banker's home and trying to budge the stay-put with sweet reason, stern reprimands and harsh threats, in that order. When this failed, Waterbury sent for his deputies; he wasn't about to pull a gun in the Hinchley's front hallway, and

111

he lacked the strength to remove Max bodily. Prowse and Dagget handled that chore, with scant regard for Max's dignity.

In the morning, Logantown buzzed with talk of the prophet's latest escapade. Rumors flew in and out of stores and livery stables and barber shops; Max's arrest was discussed, debated and enlarged upon to the extent that many a citizen believed he had committed assault and battery on Aaron Hinchley, had threatened Ella with a knife and fired a shot at the housemaid.

The news was broken to the Texans while they were at breakfast in the dining room of the Heenan Hotel; the cook was informative, but less inclined to exaggerate.

"The way I hear it, Fitch invited himself into the Hinchley place and started bendin' old Aaron's ear about some crazy dream he had . . ."

"About the bridge fallin' down," guessed Stretch.

"Heard about it, have you?" asked the cook.

"Hasn't everybody?" challenged Larry.

"Well, old Aaron ordered Fitch out, and Fitch stayed put," shrugged the cook. "So Aaron said as how that makes him a trespasser, and he sent the law, and now Fitch is stuck in jail."

After breakfast, the Texans were mutually agreed that the dreamer deserved a night in the poly; after all he had invaded the privacy of law-abiding citizens. Five minutes after coming to that decision, they reflected one night in jail should be punishment enough. They asked about the location of the Hinchley home and headed for the residential sector, intending to reason with the banker. If Aaron Hinchley could be dissuaded from swearing charges against Max, the dreamer could be back in his barn and tending the mare and her new foal within the hour.

As it happened, they didn't need to walk all the way to the banker's home. Hinchley and his daughter, heading for the intersection in the family surrey, were sighted and hailed by the Texans.

"They're friends of Max Fitch," said Louise, reaching for the reins.

"And mighty rough company," muttered Hinchley. "Let go, Louise, for gosh sakes. I'm quite capable of handling the team."

He stalled the rig near the sidewalk. Larry and Stretch doffed their Stetsons to Louise, nodded respectfully to her father and began their plea for leniency, Larry stressing,

"Max don't ask for anything for himself. When you get right down to it, he's frettin' for everybody else—not his own self."

"Which makes him a very unselfish gentleman," smiled Louise, "of charitable instincts."

"You can save your breath," Hinchley told Larry. "My daughter has already persuaded me to withdraw my charge against Fitch. She's convinced me I acted hastily last night." Grimacing, he added, "I only wish that wild-eyed prophet would confine his visits to business hours."

"Were you gentlemen thinking of settling in Logantown?" asked Louise.

"We never settle anyplace, Miss Louise," Stretch told her. "Just stopped by Logantown to rest our horses and play a little poker. Likely we'll be movin' out in a couple of days."

"But, while we're here, we'll keep an eye on Max," said Larry.

"Try and keep him out of trouble?" frowned Hinchley. "Great idea! Todd Waterbury should have thought of it months ago. What Fitch needs is a tight guard—day and night."

En route to the bank, Hinchley stopped by the sheriff's office and confided his decision. Waterbury nodded affably and indicated his complete agreement, while Davey Dagget chewed tobacco and oiled a shotgun, and Leroy Prowse strutted out to the waiting surrey to pay his respects to Louise. A short time later, when the Texans stopped by, Max was being released. They greeted him with reproachful frowns and, shrugging uneasily, he admitted, "I had no right to disturb the whole Hinchley household —I guess."

"What do you mean—you guess?" challenged Larry. "Hell, Max, you can't rouse folks out of their beds in the middle of the doggone night."

"It ain't decent," asserted Stretch.

"I was desperate," Max told them, as they sauntered away from the law office. "The dream came back to me last night—the same vision. I saw it so clearly—the bridge sagging. And I could hear the train-whistle, the screams of the passengers as the Pullman cars plunged into the gorge . . ."

"We should've fed him sarsaparilla last night," opined Stretch. "One stiff slug of rye

115

and he goes home and dreams up a train wreck."

"You're goin' on back to the barn now," Larry told Max; he made it sound more a command than a piece of advice. "You can't get into trouble tendin' the mare and her foal."

"Pike can manage without me," shrugged Max, "but I'll go back to the barn, if that's what you think I should do."

"That's what we think you should do," Stretch said firmly.

Max nodded absently and wandered away, and the Texans ambled downtown in search of a barber shop. At the Settlers National, Jay Taflin had surreptitiously transferred a quantity of counterfeit banknotes from his pockets to the draws of his desk, unobserved by Aaron Hinchley, who was interviewing a client in his office. Half of the fake dinero brought to Logantown by Morrison and Kilburn was now secreted at the bank. Tomorrow morning, Taflin would smuggle in the second half. And tomorrow afternoon, after Hinchley had left to join the reception committee at the railroad depot, Taflin would rig some more changes.

While the Lone Star Hellions bought shaves and haircuts, while Jay Taflin considered the pleasing prospect of quitting Logantown with Rose Dawes as his mistress, Phil Crane was playing host to the sheriff—or at least trying to. Gently but firmly, Waterbury refused the saloonkeeper's offer of an early morning shot of bourbon. He doffed his hat and nodded affably, but refused Rose Dawe's invitation to make himself at home.

"I'll stand," he told them, propping an elbow on the bar. "Don't plan on being here long enough to get Foot-weary. Just thought you'd like to know, Crane, I'll be turnin' your boys loose in a little while. They'll be back on the job by noon."

"Well now, I certainly appreciate that, Sheriff," said Crane. "Can't imagine why they attacked your deputies. I know Rafe and Jerry and Steve have always gotten along with lawmen . . ."

"I already talked it over with Davey and Leroy," drawled the sheriff. "Seems Rafe Soper and his pards jumped 'em in a side alley—and it was plenty dark in there. I guess that explains it, huh Crane?"

"Sheriff, I'm not sure I understand . . ." began Crane.

"They didn't know who they were jumpin',"

grinned Waterbury. "That plain enough for you?"

"A mistake," nodded Crane. "Yes, of course."

"Brings up an interestin' question," said Waterbury, still grinning. "Who were Soper and his pards after?"

"I wouldn't worry about it, Sheriff," said Crane. "Chances are they got a little drunk and felt like throwing their weight around. You know how it is."

"I know Steve Nash is teetotal," countered Waterbury. "He deals faro and likes to stay clear-headed. And Rafe Soper is one of your bartenders—I never yet saw him drunk. And Jerry Hyne is your bouncer. He needs to stay sober while he's on the job." He leaned forward to prod Crane's chest with a forefinger. "Wouldn't like to believe you sent 'em out, Crane. Know what I mean, don't you? If, for instance, a couple of sports got lucky last night and took you for a few thousand, and you decided to get it back—the easy way."

"Well, damn it, Sheriff," blustered Crane. "If you're hinting I'd order my men to—to do a thing like that . . ."

"When you've toted a badge as long as I

have, you get to suspectin' everybody," shrugged Waterbury. Poker-faced, he added, "Even saloonkeepers."

"I assure you . . ." began Crane.

"You don't have to assure me of anything," shrugged the sheriff. "Didn't come here to make accusations. Just came to tell you Soper and his pards have slept deep and hearty. I'll send 'em back to you purty soon. Reckon I can count on you to keep 'em in line." As he turned away from the bar, he nodded to Rose again. "You're lookin' mighty serious this mornin', Miss Rose. Lady as purty as you ought to smile oftener."

From the Wheel Of Fortune, the boss-lawman returned to his office in expectation of a quiet day. So much for his hopes, he had barely settled himself into a caneback on the office porch, had barely got started on his whittling, when two important citizens came hustling across from the opposite sidewalk. The heftier of the two was Gus Ashworth, Logantown's mayor. The runty jasper in shirtsleeves was Orville Hardy, the telegrapher.

Florid with fury, the mayor climbed to the porch and brandished a slip of paper in Waterbury's face.

"Take a look at this, Todd! Take a good look! By Judas, this time he's gone *too* far!"

"Mornin', Gus," nodded Waterbury. "Mornin', Orv. What you got there, Gus? Telegram for me?"

"It's addressed to the president of the railroad!" raged the mayor. "Fitch just now dictated this message to Orv and told him to send it off to the headquarters of Trans-West! And he had the bare-faced gall to name *me* as the sender!"

"You sayin' you didn't give Fitch permission to . . . ?"

"That damn fool Fitch said nothing to me! The first I heard of it was when Orv came to me to check on it!"

"Didn't seem right, Sheriff," interjected the telegrapher. "Fitch acted kind of furtive, you know? I asked was he sure Mayor Ashworth wanted the message sent, and he said sure enough and get a hustle on."

"Message says as how the bridge across Garvie's Gorge is gonna collapse any tick of the clock," observed Waterbury, as he stowed the telegram in a pocket.

"If Orv hadn't thought to check with me,"

growled Ashworth, "if he'd gone ahead and transmitted the message . . ."

"But he didn't," shrugged Waterbury.

"If he had," said Ashworth, "we'd have become the laughing-stock of the whole Trans-West route."

"You swearin' out a complaint, Gus?" asked Waterbury.

"You're damn right I am," declared Ashworth. "It's high time we sent Fitch away —far from Logantown . . ."

"To a territorial prison?" frowned Waterbury. "Takin' this a mite strong, aren't you, Gus? Boy means no harm. He has these dreams and . . ."

"And keeps on scaring the daylights out of law-abiding citizens," scowled Ashworth.

"Signing somebody else's name to a telegram —that's breaking the law, Sheriff," the telegrapher pointed out. "Mayor Ashworth says I should report it to my head office."

"If Western Union decides to sue Fitch, he's finished," said Ashworth. "We'll be rid of him for good and all."

"I don't know if the boy meant any real harm, Gus," argued Waterbury.

"What are you waiting for, Todd" challenged

121

Ashworth. "You have your duty. *Do* it, damnitall!"

"All right, Gus, all right," sighed Waterbury. "No need to get your gizzard all tangled up." He called to Deputy Prowse, who emerged from the office in eager anticipation. "Been listenin', have you, Leroy?"

"Let me handle it," begged Prowse. "Let me bring Fitch in."

"Go ahead," nodded Waterbury. "But you don't have to rough him up. He's harmless."

"That's a matter of opinion," growled the mayor.

Ten minutes later, the Happy Haven was again in charge of Pike Hewson, and Max Fitch was languishing in the county jail; the sole occupant, now that Crane's hirelings had been released.

From the barber shop, Larry and Stretch ambled to Colley Road and the Happy Haven, expecting to pass the time of day with Max and the taciturn Pike. They had to settle for a few terse words from Pike, who informed them of his boss's arrest.

"That ain't news," Stretch pointed out. "We knew he got arrested, and we were there when they turned him loose."

"That was the first time," countered Pike.

"The first time?" prodded Larry.

"He got arrested again, just a little while ago," said Pike.

"Sonofagun!" breathed Stretch.

"What in tarnation did he do *this* time?" demanded Larry.

"Tried to wire the boss of the railroad," shrugged Pike. "Tried to talk the operator into puttin' Mayor Ashworth's name to the telegram."

"Damn and blast . . ." mumbled Larry, as he trudged out of the barn.

"Why d'you suppose he . . . ?" began Stretch.

"I aim to ask him!" scowled Larry.

When they strode into Waterbury's office a short time later, the wily old Sheriff accorded them careful courtesy and frowned a warning to the bumptious Leroy Prowse, who triumphantly asserted,

"Your lame-brained friend is back where he belongs."

"We heard," said Stretch.

Davey Dagget, from his prone position on the office couch, eyed the Texans curiously and remarked,

"Beats me why a couple hombres like you —drifters passin' through—would care a damn about a plumb peculiar feller like little Max."

"Maybe he acts peculiar, but that don't mean he's crazy," argued Larry. In a few brisk sentences, he recounted his experience of the night before, describing how he beat the wheel at Crane's with Max calling his bets. "If everybody was *that* crazy," he finished, "every big shot gambler in Logantown would have to pack up and quit."

"He was just lucky is all," insisted Prowse.

Waterbury, who had been listening intently, now thought to enquire,

"Where'd you boys go after you cleaned up at the Wheel Of Fortune?"

Larry eyed him blankly.

"Why would you want to know that?" he demanded.

"When Sheriff Waterbury asks a question . . ." began Prowse.

"Hush up, Leroy," chided the sheriff. "Valentine, I'm askin' a fair question and I got my reasons. Which way'd you head?"

"Along the main stem and into the alley that leads to the Heenan Hotel," shrugged Larry.

"Only we didn't get to the hotel rightaway," offered Stretch. "Got side-tracked kind of."

"Stopped by to visit with Doc Milford," said Larry.

He wondered why the sheriff chuckled, and Waterbury wasn't about to offer any explanations; he had just solved the riddle of why three plug-uglies from the Wheel Of Fortune had attacked his deputies. In the gloom of the alley and at a slight distance, Prowse and Dagget could be—obviously *had* been—mistaken for Larry and Stretch.

"You hombres drink any of Doc Milford's booze?" asked Dagget.

"Plenty," said Larry.

"Proves you got courage," grunted Dagget. "Man has to be brave to take a shot of Doc's fire-water."

Impatiently, Larry unstrapped his gunbelt and tossed his hardware onto Waterbury's desk. Stretch followed his example and, shrugging and grinning, the sheriff assured them,

"If you want to visit with Max, it's okay by me." He nodded to Prowse. "Open up for 'em, Leroy."

"Five minutes is all you get, hear?" growled

125

Prowse, as he unlocked the cellblock entrance. "Five minutes—and not a second longer."

"Take ten, fifteen minutes if you want," Waterbury offered the Texans.

"Damnitall, Todd . . ." began Prowse, turning red.

"Just rap on the door when you want out," said Waterbury.

"Yeah, sure," nodded Larry. "Much obliged."

He strode into the jailhouse with Stretch tagging him. The door clanged shut behind them, and Prowse glared indignantly at his chief.

"You shouldn't have talked me down that way," he chided. "I told 'em five minutes. A lawman ought never humiliate his deputy in front of strangers."

"Better it should be *me* humiliates you, Leroy," countered Waterbury. "You keep pushin' Valentine and Emerson and you'll end up wishin' you'd never pinned on a star."

"Valentine and Emerson?" Dagget raised his brows. "Them two? They're Larry and Stretch—those proddy Texans I been hearin' about?"

"*I* never heard of 'em," declared Prowse.

"Gives me kind of a warm feelin' inside,"

Waterbury confided to Dagget, while staring wistfully at the cellblock door. "I recognized 'em right off, when we broke up that hassle yesterday. No wonder Burchell and his three pards got the worst of it. They were licked before they started."

"You talk as if you *admire* those saddle-tramps," complained Prowse.

"I can afford to admire 'em now," grinned Waterbury. "I'm about to be pastured out. And, by golly, I aim to go peaceful, aim to turn in my badge while I still got my health and my nerve and my sense of humor—which I'd damn soon lose if I locked horns with Larry and Stretch."

In the jailhouse corridor, the Texans rolled and lit cigarettes and stared through the bars at Max, who perched on the edge of his bunk and showed them a worried frown.

"Why?" challenged Larry. "Just tell me *why*."

"And keep it plain and simple," urged Stretch, "so I can savvy what you're gabbin' about."

"I'm neither a fool nor a fraud, Larry," said Max. "What could I gain by disrupting the railroad's schedule? Why should I beg them to stop

127

using the bridge at Garvie's Gorge, if I wasn't sure—absolutely certain—it's defective? It *will* fall, Larry. It will fall under the weight of a train bound east or west, and there'll be heavy loss of life." He matched Larry's stare a long moment, then grimly assured him, "I'd do anything to prevent such a tragedy—anything at all."

"You've been wrong before," Larry reminded him.

"More often right than wrong," retorted Max. "Have you forgotten last night—the roulette wheel at Crane's?"

"Little feller, we ain't about to forget *that*," declared Stretch.

"All right." Larry shrugged resignedly. "We owe you, Max."

"No obligation," shrugged Max.

"Even so," insisted Larry. "Anybody does us a kindness, we like to show our appreciation."

"There's little you can do for me anyway," opined Max. "Apparently I fractured some Federal law by trying to persuade the telegrapher to put Mayor Ashworth's name to a telegram—without his permission."

"Got law and order in Logantown, haven't you?" challenged Larry. "That means you have to stand trial. A man's entitled to his day in court."

"Well—I guess so . . ."

"And a smart lawyer could maybe talk a jury into turnin' you loose. He could make the judge —and everybody else—listen to *your* side of the story, tell 'em *why* you tried to reach the railroad bosses."

"A jury trial?" Max stroked his chin and nodded pensively. "Yes, with a jury, I might have a chance. Especially if Doc Allgood or Slim McBride could be sworn in as jurymen."

"How come?" prodded Stretch.

"Well, they might influence the other jurors," said Max. "Doc Allgood would be bound to remember the time I saved his life . . ."

"You talkin' about the young doctor—same feller Doc Milford told us about last night?" frowned Larry.

"He's young and enthusiastic," said Max. "He'll travel anywhere—any time—to tend a patient."

"How'd you save his life?"

"He was about to drive out of town, headed for a trapper's camp in the mountains. I warned him against using the short-cut through Ventura Pass . . ."

"Why? Another vision?"

"A premonition, yes. I predicted an avalanche at the approximate time Doc Allgood would have been passing through. He decided to heed my warning, took the long route up the mountainside to Arrowhead Rock. From up there he could see clear to the pass."

"And?"

"There *was* an avalanche. He saw the pass fill in."

"And this other feller—McBride?"

"He's a ranch-hand works for the Rocking J outfit. We met along the southeast trail while I was on my way to the Gaffney farm. He told me he'd been ordered to flush strays out of the high brush in Rocking J's east quarter, and he'd be using the line-shack on Taggart's Ridge. I warned him to stay clear of that shack, because I'd seen it struck by lightning . . ."

"There was a storm?"

"Not while I was talking to McBride. The storm came a day later. But I'd already seen the shack wrecked . . ."

"In a dream?"

"And what happened to McBride?"

130

"He was sheltering in the shack when the storm began. My warning must have made him nervous. Anyway, he got out of there, saddled his horse and started riding down from the ridge. He'd travelled only about sixty yards, he told me, when the lightning flashed. He looked back, saw the shack burst into flames . . ."

"With McBride and the doc on the jury, you'd stand a better than even chance of an acquittal," Larry opined.

"Spooky is what I call it," muttered Stretch, eyeing Max askance. "Him and his visions."

"We owe him," said Larry.

"Sure, we owe him," nodded Stretch. "So now what?"

"I got a hunch about that sheriff," said Larry. "The bonehead deputy . . ."

"Prowse," interjected Max.

"He acts proddy all the time," said Larry, "but the sheriff stays gentle and sociable. I think he'd listen to reason."

"What exactly do you have in mind?" asked Max.

"We're gonna find you a lawyer," Larry told him. "And maybe I can talk the sheriff into turnin' you loose, so you can keep the Happy Haven in operation."

"I'd appreciate that," frowned Max. "Larry, are you asking Sheriff Waterbury to release me into your custody?"

"Somethin' like that," said Larry. "Maybe he'll buy it and maybe he won't. Only one way to find out."

Despite Deputy Prowse's vehement protests, Todd Waterbury lent an attentive and receptive ear to Larry's request and agreed there was little to be gained by keeping Max Fitch under lock and key from now till the coming of the circuit judge. But he offered a stern warning.

"You'd be responsible for him, Valentine."

"It wouldn't be the first time we played bodyguard," drawled Stretch.

"No," agreed Waterbury. "But young Max is somethin' special. You'll have to keep your eyes on him every minute. He's got a bee in his bonnet about Garvie's Gorge and, by golly, if he makes one more wrong move . . ."

"We'll guard him close," Larry promised. "First we find him a lawyer, then we take him back to the barn. Between now and the trial, one of us'll be stickin' as close as Max's own skin."

"Ridley Hotel's the best place to find a lawyer," offered Waterbury. "It's close by the courthouse. We got three-four lawyers in Logan County, all bachelors, all livin' at the Ridley. Young Max can look 'em over and make his choice."

Within the quarter-hour, the dreamer had been released into the custody of the Lone Star Hellions, who walked him uptown toward the Ridley Hotel and yet another crisis, the worst Max Fitch would ever experience.

5

THREE men lounged in the alley beside the Ridley Hotel and tried to appear casual and disinterested, as Max and the Texans approached. Jake Thornley, the B-Bar foreman, swore softly and darted a glance toward the rear of the alley, while Cardew and Hale traded comments.

"Still hangin' around," Cardew observed. "Them smart-aleck saddlebums."

"Looks like they got 'emselves a new friend," muttered Hale.

"No skin off our noses," said Thornley. "Just so long as they walk on past. We ain't here for another ruckus."

"They ain't walkin' on past," warned Cardew. The three withdrew into the alley, as the Texans passed the entrance and stepped up to the porch of the hotel. "Jake—I think they're goin' inside."

"Well—what of it?" challenged Thornley.

The names of guests using their rooms as business offices were listed on a board nailed by the hotel entrance. Max paused there to study the list and swap opinions with his bodyguards, while the B-Bar men listened intently.

"There's Abner Gault—said to be the best lawyer in the whole territory," Max remarked. "But he's inclined to charge a heavy fee. A man of very expensive tastes is Mister Gault."

"No matter," said Larry. "We can afford him."

"No." Max shook his head vehemently. "I won't let you use all the cash you won last night. I'd as soon pay my own lawyer, but I'll choose a man whose charges are reasonable." He consulted the list again. "There's John T. Phelan. I think he specializes in land transactions."

"Only one other lawyer there," Larry noted. "S.D. Parrant."

"Oh, sure. Sam Parrant," nodded Max. "I guess he'd be as reliable as Mister Gault, but not as expensive."

"Room Five, second floor," observed Stretch. "Okay, Maxie boy, let's go on up and chew the fat with Mister Parrant."

As Max and his tall protectors moved into the lobby, Thornley eyed his companions nervously.

"You heard?" he challenged.

"We heard," nodded Cardew. "And I'm thinkin' they better not find Parrant—not yet. Maybe Al is still up there."

"We'll have to stall 'em," Thornley said bluntly, "and I mean *now*!"

He hustled up to the porch with Cardew and Hale in tow and barged into the lobby just as Max and the Texans were - moving past the reception desk and approaching the stairs. Grim-faced and truculent, the ramrod bounded across the lobby to reach the stairs ahead of the trio. He turned to confront them, his fists bunched. Stretch glanced over his shoulder at Cardew and Hale, nudged Larry and remarked,

"We didn't beat all the sass out of this bunch. Seems like they've come back for more."

"Saddletramp," scowled Thornley, "we got a little score to settle with you!"

"Hey, what's this all about?" demanded the desk-clerk, looking up from his newspaper. "Listen, gents, we don't want any trouble in here."

Ignoring the clerk, Thornley gestured toward the entrance and growled a command at the Texans.

"Outside. Move!"

"Get goin', Beanpole," ordered Hale.

He came up behind Stretch, grasped at his shoulders and tried to turn him and shove him away from the stairs. But the taller Texan didn't budge. Hale cursed and shoved harder and Stretch spun nimbly, his bunched right flashing out like a piston, slamming into the vulnerable section above Hale's buckle. Hale back-stepped, clutching at his midriff and gasping frantically, while Larry moved forward and cleared the way for Max. Left shoulder down, right fist drawn back, he charged Thornley and drove him hard against the stair-rail. Thornley cursed and tried to get his hands to Larry's throat, and then he was yelling wildly; Larry's devastating jab, delivered at short range, had thrown him clear over the rail. He somersaulted and crashed to the floor and, whirling to meet Cardew's rush, Larry growled a command to the startled Max.

"Go on up and talk to the lawyer. If the sheriff finds you mixed into a ruckus, you'll be jail-bait again."

He grunted a curse as Cardew's fist bounced off the side of his head. The blow flung him sideways to trip and sprawl across Thornley, who was lurching groggily to his feet until that

137

moment. Stretch yelled a warning and ducked, as Hale caught his breath, picked up a chair and charged. The clerk protested urgently and vaulted his desk.

"The management will sue for damages!" he warned, making a grab for the chair.

Stretch stepped in close and clobbered Hale while he was raising the chair. Hale, the chair and the clerk went down in a tangled heap, and then Stretch was bounding across to lend aid to Larry, who had struggled upright to trade blows with Cardew, while Thornley clung to his legs and tried to bring him down again. For a moment, Max hesitated. The logic of Larry's command could not be denied. If he became involved in this fracas, Sheriff Waterbury might well decide that he would be safer behind bars; he didn't relish being arrested three times in the one day.

Law and order arrived in person of Leroy Prowse. The bumptious deputy had followed Max and his bodyguards at a distance after they took their leave of the jailhouse; he meant to keep an eye on the dreamer, to miss no chance of re-arresting him. Out of circulation, Max Fitch could hardly compete with Prowse in his courtship of Louise Hinchley—or so Prowse believed. With that thought in mind, he had tagged the Texans and their charge all the way from Waterbury's office.

"Don't just stand there, Deputy!" chided the clerk. "*Do* something!"

"Where's Crazy Max?" demanded Prowse.

He stepped into the lobby, eager for his first glimpse of the dreamer, while the clerk picked himself up and sidled clear of the Texans and their assailants.

"Never mind Crazy Max!" he panted. "Break up this fight—before they wreck the place!"

"Where is he?" snapped Prowse.

"He went upstairs," frowned the clerk. "I heard his friend say 'go talk to the lawyer'— but I don't know which lawyer." Prowse made for the stairs, but hesitated at the clerk's urgent plea. "You can't walk away from this—this riot! Max Fitch isn't causing any trouble. The trouble is right here before your eyes—so what the devil are you waiting for?" He gasped a protest, as Prowse drew his Colt. "Hey! Don't fire that thing in here!"

"You B-Bar men!" boomed Prowse. "I order you—in the name of the law . . . !"

He wasn't given time to finish the command. Cardew, sent reeling by a blow from Stretch, collided with him and threw him off-balance. Again the clerk scuttled clear, and the deputy hit the floor with a resounding thud and a violent oath. And then, as he began struggling to his feet, he raised his eyes to the first floor landing and saw Max Fitch standing there, pallid and trembling, beckoning urgently. Rightaway Prowse's gaze fastened on the thing gripped in Max's right hand—a knife—the blade red.

"Hold it right there!" he ordered.

Max stood frozen, his mouth working, but his voice choked off, while Prowse climbed toward him, his Colt at the ready. In the lobby, the Texans still traded blows with the three hard cases, gradually forcing them to the entrance and out to the porch.

Reaching Max, Prowse brandished the cocked Colt in his face and growled a command.

"Drop that knife!"

Max found his voice.

"*What* knife?"

"Right there in your hand, you damn fool!" snarled Prowse. "Who'd you use it on, dreamer? Who'd you kill?"

"Kill? *I* didn't kill him!" Max dropped the knife and flinched, as Prowse rammed the Colt into his belly. "It must've happened—just before I reached his office . . ."

"Whose office?"

"Mister Parrant's."

"Stand by the wall a moment, dreamer." Prowse waited for Max to obey, then bent and picked up the knife. Grimacing at the blood-wet blade, he vowed, "You'll hang for this."

"For pity's sake, Deputy, you have to believe me . . . !"

"Always knew you'd go too far. Dangerous you are, Fitch. Just like I told Miss Louise and her pa—a fool like you oughtn't be allowed roam the streets. And now you've proved I was right."

"I swear to you . . . !"

"Get moving, Fitch! Along the corridor to Parrant's office."

In a daze, Max stumbled ahead of the deputy's levelled gun, along the corridor toward the open door of the room rented by Sam Parrant.

The second deputy now appeared out front of the hotel, arriving just in time to see the last wild blows of that short and violent affray. And, as Dagget paused by the porch, Al Burchell emerged from the side alley, scowling at his battered cronies and bellowing a reprimand. Thornley left the porch in undignified fashion; Larry's swinging uppercut drove him over the verandah rail to crash to the sidewalk. Simultaneously, Stretch got behind Hale and landed a kick to his backside. Hale hurtled forward, flopped to the steps and collapsed beside Thornley. And then, as both Texans turned on Cardew, that toilworn hard case raised his hands in surrender.

"All right . . . !" he panted. "I've had enough."

From the hotel entrance, the clerk aimed a tirade of complaint at Dagget, demanding the arrest of all five brawlers. But Dagget, who regarded the arrest of street-brawlers as a waste of good time, retorted,

"I'd as soon run 'em outa town, Clarence. You tell me who started it, and I'll bar 'em from Logantown for twenty-four hours."

"You realize what you're saying, Deputy Dagget?" challenged the clerk. "It's as good as guaranteeing there'll be another bullabaloo twenty-four hours from now."

"I'll be responsible for my men, Dagget," frowned Burchell. "They had their orders. I told 'em to stay clear of those Texans . . ."

"Don't seem like they paid you no mind," observed Dagget. "Seems like they got their comeuppance." He grinned unsympathetically as he added, "Again."

"Head on up to Hanahan's Bar," Burchell ordered his men. "You get just one shot of whiskey for the road, and then I'm takin' you back to the spread—to work." He gestured brusquely. "Move."

Ignoring the Texans, he nodded so-long to Dagget and fell in behind Thornley and Cardew and Hale, who trudged wearily away from the hotel. Dagget clamped his teeth about a cigar and scratched a match. He was puffing on the Long 9 and trading stares with the Texans, when his colleague bellowed to him from a second storey window.

"Hey, Dagget, fetch the sheriff! I'm arresting Fitch—for the murder of Sam Parrant!"

Dagget blinked incredulously, then turned on his heel and dashed back toward the law office. The desk-clerk eyed the Texans nervously, as they strode past him and into the lobby.

"What'd he say? Did he say—murder?"

Larry didn't pause to answer the clerk's question. Tagged by Stretch, he climbed the stairs three at a time. They were guided to the open doorway of the dead lawyer's room by a familiar voice raised in frantic protest.

"You can't arrest me? Why me? I'm completely innocent—incapable of—of doing *this*—to *any* man . . ."

They reached the open doorway and sized up the situation—Max sitting in a chair in the corner nearest the open window, wearing Prowse's manacles and a harassed expression—Prowse perched on a corner of the desk, hefting his .45 and looking grimly triumphant—the body of Sam Parrant sprawled face-down in front of the desk, blood staining the back of his shirt.

"He'll hang," Prowse smugly predicted. "Just as sure as there's green grass in Wyoming, he'll hang."

"Larry—Stretch—I assure you . . ." began Max.

"Don't get any rash notions, you two," warned Prowse, covering them with the .45. "Your crazy friend is my prisoner."

"Don't *you* get rash, badge-toter," scowled Stretch. "I'm liable to take that hogleg off of you and ram the muzzle-end down your gullet."

"Prowse, you keep pointin' that thing at us

and you'll find more trouble than you can handle," growled Larry.

Prowse glowered at him resentfully, but took the hint; he uncocked the Colt and let the muzzle dip.

"Remember," he breathed. "Fitch is my prisoner."

"This is ridiculous," protested Max. "They call me crazy, but, damnitall, *Prowse* is the crazy one!"

"Shuddup—killer!" snapped Prowse.

"Max, you want to tell us what happened here?" prodded Larry.

"Who invited *you* to ask questions" challenged Prowse. "*I'm* the arresting officer. *I'll* handle this investigation."

"Sounded like a fair question anyway." This observation was voiced by Sheriff Waterbury, who entered the room slowly, a mite short of breath after his hurried journey from his office. Behind him, Dagget filled the doorway and turned to disperse the curious locals jamming the corridor. "That's right, Davey, send 'em about their business." The boss-lawman trudged to a chair and seated himself, showing no revulsion for the body sprawled near his feet; it wasn't Todd Waterbury's first sight of a murdered man. "I oughtn't hustle upstairs that way. Young Doc Allgood says it ain't wise for a man my age."

"Just wanted you to see what I found here, Sheriff," drawled Prowse, sheathing his Colt. "I got the situation well and truly in hand—arrested the guilty party—found the murder-weapon . . ."

"How about witnesses?" asked Waterbury.

"Yeah," grunted Stretch. "How about that?"

"Listen—do we have to stand for all this back-talk?" Prowse appealed to his chief. "This is a job for the law. We don't want any smart-mouthed trouble-shooters buying in."

"It's our fault Max came to this hotel," Larry informed the sheriff. "When we quit your office, we were gonna find him a lawyer—remember?"

"So you brought him right here to the Ridley Hotel," nodded Waterbury. "And then what?"

"We got prodded into a ruckus with Burchell's sidekicks," said Larry. "I didn't want Max mixed into it, so I sent him up here to find the lawyer."

"Fitch came up here and killed Parrant," declared Prowse. "That's the way it had to be!"

"Make that plainer, Leroy," invited Waterbury,. "Tell us what you saw."

"I heard the ruckus downstairs and came in to investigate," said Prowse. "The clerk told me Valentine had sent Fitch upstairs. Well, when I reached the stairs and looked up, I saw Fitch on the landing . . ." He picked up the blood-stained knife from the desk-top, "holding this —and looking guilty as hell."

"He had the knife?" frowned Waterbury.

"Gripped in his right hand," declared Prowse, seizing the murder-weapon by its hilt. "Like so."

"Not much of a knife," Dagget commented. "My guess'd be Parrant used it to open his mail —when he got any mail."

"Paper knife," nodded Waterbury.

"Even so," Dagget conceded, "it sure did the job."

"Sure did the job," agreed Waterbury, glancing at the body.

"I hustled up the stairs, disarmed the killer and arrested him," bragged Prowse. "Brought him back here and confronted him with his handiwork."

"This is insane," groaned Max. "Oh, Lord! *Somebody* has to try and *understand* . . . !"

147

"Try me, son," urged Waterbury.

"Go ahead, Max," said Larry. "Just tell it slow and calm—the truth."

Max's agitation increased. He stared wildly at Larry and complained,

"That's the hell of it! They'll never believe me! You heard how Prowse talked! He's not interested in truth . . . !"

"Slow and calm," insisted Larry.

"He's tongue-tied," jeered Prowse. "Guilty and scared stiff."

"One more yap outa you, and *you'll* get to be stiff," warned Stretch, "all the way from your fat head to your big feet."

"Listen, you . . . !" gasped Prowse.

"Simmer down, Leroy," ordered Waterbury, staring hard at the prisoner. "I'm still waitin' to hear Max's side of it." Gently he assured Max, "You got a right to be heard, boy."

"What use," sighed Max, "if nobody will believe me?"

"Tell it anyway," said Waterbury.

Max shrugged helplessly and bowed his head, his troubled gaze on his manacled wrists.

"I came upstairs," he told them. "I found Mister Parrant's room and knocked at the door. There was no answer, but the door was unlocked, so I opened it and came in . . ." He heaved another sigh. "The worst mistake of my life."

"Go on," urged Waterbury.

"He was lying—just as you see him now," said Max. "I didn't try to move him. I had—no way of knowing if he were dead—or still breathing. All I could see was the knife—and all that blood. I realize—now—I shouldn't have touched it. But, when I was a boy, I saw a steer with an arrow in its side, and I've never forgotten how a ranch-hand hurried to draw the arrow out. That was back in Nesbitt, Kansas. Starving Indians used to raid the ranches to steal beef . . ."

"You sayin' the knife was in Parrant's back, and you pulled it out?" challenged Dagget.

"That's how it happened," said Max. "And then—not realizing I was still holding the knife —I dashed out to find help. I still wasn't sure if he were dead or alive."

"Hogwash!" snorted Prowse. "He was making a run for it—looking for a way out. I challenged him from below the stairs and I'm telling you he was near crazy from fear and guilt!"

"He must've been attacked—just before I found him," muttered Max.

"You pass anybody in the corridor?" demanded Waterbury. Max shook his head. "You dead sure there wasn't anybody else in the room?"

"Just Mister Parrant—and me," said Max.

"Did you open that?" asked Larry, frowning at the window. "Or was it open when you came in?"

"Waterbury, are you gonna let this drifter take over the whole damn investigation?" challenged Prowse.

"Call me 'Sheriff'," said Waterbury, softly but warningly.

Prowse made to hurl a bitter retort, but thought better of it. He took a deep breath, glowered at Larry a moment, then asked Waterbury,

"Are you thinking of pinning badges on Valentine and his skinny sidekick—Sheriff?"

"Can't be done," Waterbury said with a bland grin. "Haven't you heard, Leroy? The Texas Hell-Raisers ain't partial to tin stars." He eyed Max expectantly. "What about the window, boy?"

"I don't remember. I didn't notice." Max

shook his head in confusion. "Maybe it was open when I came in. I'm not sure of anything any more."

"The real killer could've gotten out that way," Larry suggested.

"What do you mean—'real killer'?" scowled Prowse. He pointed accusingly at Max. "*There's* the real killer." With his jaw jutting aggressively, he strode to the window and glanced into the back alley. "No balcony," he announced, "and no fire-stairs. No way anybody could reach this window from outside."

"How about with a ladder?" asked Dagget.

"We're a couple stories up," countered Prowse. "I don't know anybody owns a ladder *that* long." Turning to face them again, he nodded emphatically and declared, "Fitch is our man. There are no two ways about it."

"I didn't do it," mumbled Max.

"*Why* would he do it?" Larry asked Waterbury. "A man don't kill for no reason at all. Max scarce even knew this Parrant hombre. Ain't that so, Max?"

"He rented a horse from my barn a couple times is all," shrugged Max.

"A lunatic needs no motives," insisted

151

Prowse. "We all know Fitch is crazy—him and his wild dreams."

"Looks bad for you, son," Waterbury said dolefully. "I guess you realize that—or don't you?"

"It wouldn't be—the first time . . ." Max stared worriedly at the still figure. "Not the first time—an innocent man was accusesd on the basis of circumstantial evidence."

"You'll get every break I can give you—without dishonorin' my badge," Waterbury promised. "Davey, you send for the undertaker, then start checkin' around. I want to know if any citizen on that side of town . . ." He gestured to the window, "saw anybody tryin' to climb out of this room."

"That wouldn't make sense," argued Prowse. "Any fool who tried to get out that window—he'd be down there in the alley now, with his neck broken."

"You take Max to jail," ordered Waterbury. "And no rough stuff, Leroy. Just lock him in a cell and do it gentle. He won't give you any trouble."

"Heaven help him if he does," grinned Prowse. "On your feet—killer."

"Prowse, we'll be visitin' Max in a little

152

while," warned Larry, as Max stood up. "If I see any bruises on him, you'd better start practicin' how to duck."

"Now, see here . . . !" began Prowse.

"Just take him out, Leroy," sighed Waterbury. "Just take him out."

After Prowse had left with the prisoner, after the undertaker and his helper had taken the body away, Waterbury began puttering about the room, rummaging in the desk drawers, checking the file cabinet, wandering across to stare out the window. The Texans stayed by the closed door, smoking, busy with their own thoughts.

"Parrant's practice wasn't worth a hill of beans," the lawman confided to them. "He was never my idea of a square shooter, if you know what I mean." He squatted on the window-ledge, fished out a cigar and began patting his pockets in search of a match. Larry ambled across to give him a light. He grunted his thanks and squinted down into the back alley again. "Be that as it may, he just got himself knifed to death, and I'm still sheriff of this here territory. Still got my duty, and aim to do it."

"You think Max killed him?"

Larry spoke quietly and dispassionately. To

Waterbury, it sounded like a casual question, not a challenge.

"So far," he replied, "Max is the only suspect I got."

"Uh huh," grunted Larry.

"If he ain't guilty of murder, he's guilty of somethin' else," declared Waterbury.

"Sure," nodded Larry. "Plain foolishness. Pullin' that knife out of the lawyer's back, lettin' Prowse see him with it, is the dumbest thing little Max ever did."

"It could put a rope round his neck," Waterbury pointed out.

"Speakin' for myself, I never took kindly to the notion of a feller gettin' hung for somebody else's killin'," drawled Larry.

Stretch trudged across to join them and said, flatly,

"Max *couldn't* do it."

"You're that sure?" prodded Waterbury.

"There's a certain type of hombre that couldn't kill—not even to save his own life," asserted Stretch. "Max is that kind of hombre."

"He's got you convinced," Waterbury observed. "You've only known him a couple days, but you're bettin' he's innocent."

Larry, after a pensive scrutiny of the rear

alley, thrust his head and shoulders through the window and twisted to stare up to the roof. Then, turning again, he scanned the area east of the alley. As though reading his mind, Waterbury remarked,

"Nothin' much over thataway. Just a mess of old shacks nobody uses any more. Grain warehouse and the old tradin' post are gonna be torn down. Ain't safe to go in there. A roof is apt to fall on you." Eyeing Larry sidelong, he asked, "Does that give you any ideas?"

Before answering, Larry thrust his head out again, this time to check the other windows. Two overlooked a gallery from whence firestairs led down to the alley.

"From that gallery, any healthy jasper could reach the roof," he told Waterbury. "All he needed was a good rope. A regular rawhide lariat'd do it."

"Keep talkin'," offered Waterbury. "I ain't sayin' I'm convinced, but you might's well try."

"Not much chance he'd be sighted from this side of the hotel," said Larry. "Not if there's nobody livin' over there." He gestured to the disused buildings, then jerked a thumb upward. "So he makes it to the roof, unhitches his rope and moves along till he's directly atop this window. Take a look up there. You'll see a beam pokin' out."

Waterbury took a look, nodded clamly.

"Yeah. And so?"

"That's how he got in—and out again. Caught his loop on the end of the beam, slid down his rope and swung in through this window."

"Stabbed Parrant with his own knife . . ."

"Then climbed out the window and up the rope. When he reached the roof, all he had to do was unhitch his loop and hustle along to the gallery. A strong man, movin' fast, could've gotten out of here and down to the alley in two-three minutes."

"All right." Waterbury nodded slowly. "I'll allow you've explained how somebody else could've killed Parrant. That ain't enough to save Max Fitch's neck, but it's a start. Only we'll need more, Valentine, a whole lot more."

"Yeah, sure," agreed Larry. "We need a reason for this killin'—and the jasper that *had* that reason."

"Parrant wasn't real popular," shrugged Waterbury, "but I don't know any citizen hereabouts could profit from killin' him." Abruptly, he turned away from the widow. "Got to be gettin' back to the office now. If you boys want to hang around and dig a little deeper, I can't stop you. Just one thing." As they followed him from the room, he put a hand on Larry's arm. "Don't lock horns with Leroy—not if you can help it. You clobber a badge-toter, and I got no choice but to arrest you."

"We'll be keepin' our noses clean," Stretch grimly assured him. "Can't do much for little Max if we're fillin' cells in the same calaboose."

When they moved through the inquisitive crowd in the lobby and reached the street, they were met by Davey Dagget, who reported,

"Doc Torrance checked Parrant's body at the funeral parlor."

"Well, that's the regular routine," shrugged Waterbury. "Any fool could see how Parrant died, but there has to be a medical inspection and a death certificate."

"Doc Torrance says that one jab of the knife was all it took," offered Dagget. He stroked his jowls and traded stares with his chief and the Texans. "Kinda hard to believe, huh? I mean —little Max rammin' that knife into Parrant's back—hard enough to kill him."

"It's hard to believe, but it's all we got," said the sheriff, "until somebody comes up with

157

somethin' better." He nodded so-long to the Texans. "Come by and talk, any time you want."

"We'll be seein' you," Larry assured him.

The Texans stood quiet, rolling cigarettes and watching the lawmen head back to the jail-house. As he scratched a match, Stretch opined,

"We ought to go on back to the Happy Haven and talk to Pike."

"I guess," nodded Larry.

"Somebody has to tell him his boss got arrested again," frowned Stretch. "And, besides, he's lived around these parts quite a spell. Maybe he knows some hombre that wanted this lawyer-feller dead."

"Somebody has to know somethin'," declared Larry. "I got me a feelin', if we keep on nosin' around, askin' questions, we'll hit pay-dirt. Only one way we can pull Max out of this mess."

"Uh huh—only one way," agreed Stretch. "We just have to find the galoot that *really* did it. Well . . ." He shrugged resignedly, "here we go again."

They were disinterested in the pudgy man who crossed their path as they made for Colley

Road, and the feeling was mutual. Jay Taflin had never heard of the Lone Star Hellions. A short time before he had asked Aaron Hinchley's permission to step out for a few moments. During those few moments, he had visited Morrison and Kilburn in their quarters above the Wheel Of Fortune's barroom and collected another five bundles of counterfeit bills. Returning to the bank, he relieved Hinchley at the counter and attended a couple of clients. Not until he was sure his actions would pass unnoticed did he retreat to his desk and secrete the fake cash.

Watching from atop the batwings of an uptown saloon, Al Burchell saw the Texans part company with the lawmen and head for Colley Road. He snapped his fingers and Thornley, Cardew and Hale rose from a nearby table and followed him out to the hitch-rail where their horses awaited.

"Good timin', huh?" grinned Hale.

"We'll head on back to the spread now," muttered Burchell. "No talk till we're clear of town."

They had passed the outskirts and were making for the cattle trail, when Thornley laughed harshly and declared,

"It went better than we hoped for."

"Damn right," Burchell agreed.

"Gettin' rid of Parrant was only the half of it," grinned the ramrod. "You set Fitch up for a hangrope—and you weren't even tryin'!"

"Crazy Max'll be better dead anyway," opined Hale. "Damn fool is no use to himself nor anybody else. Just a dreamin' jackass."

"That makes it better," drawled Cardew. "Nobody looks for Crazy Max to talk sense. They'll just try him and hang him and that'll be an end of it. Meantime, Parrant can't hold no gun at our heads. What we take from the bank—it'll be all ours."

"Every last dollar of it," nodded Burchell. He grinned complacently and dug in his spurs. "Come on, let's hustle these critters. I hanker to check what's left of that dynamite—the fuses too."

For the remainder of that day, the Texans did their best to provide the Logantown law with an alternative suspect in the murder of Sam Parrant, but their efforts proved fruitless. Few locals had admired the seedy lawyer; professional gamblers and bartenders had distrusted him, and percentage-girls had given him a wide berth. Pike Hewson assured them that many a local disliked Parrant, many despised him to the point that they might have enjoyed running a knife into him. He named a few possibilities, but Larry and Stretch later learned that none of these had been anywhere near the Ridley Hotel at the time of the murder.

They visited Max in his cell after supper. He had accounted for every crumb of the meal dished up to him by Deputy Dagget.

"Got to keep up my strength," he remarked. "Daren't become weak from hunger. I'll need all my wits, a clear mind in a healthy body, to convince the judge and jury of my innocence."

"Howzat again, boy?" challenged Stretch.

"Max, you wouldn't try to be your own lawyer—would you?" frowned Larry.

"It would be more economical—conducting my own defense," said Max.

"It could cost you your life," Larry gruffly warned. "Boy, you're gonna need a sure-enough, regular, smart-talkin' lawyer. We'll hire the best . . ."

"We can afford to bide our time anyway," shrugged Max. "I don't believe the circuit judge is due for another three weeks." Squatting on the edge of his bunk, trying to keep up a brave front, he showed them a weak apology of a grin. "How are things at the Happy Haven?"

"Pike's tendin' the business," Stretch assured him. He eyed Max sadly. "Boy, it's too bad you couldn't cream your way out of this spot. Seems like you walked into it with your eyes wide open."

"I had no premonition of disaster when I knocked at Mister Parrant's door," sighed Max. "Well, there's no pattern to my dreams, Stretch. And, as you've probably been told, my predictions aren't always accurate." His face clouded over. He turned slightly to gaze up at the barred window of his cell and glimpse the stars. "A pleasant evening. The country around Garvie's Gorge looks so beautiful, so serene, this time of evening. I could almost disbelieve my dream . . ."

"He's gonna start frettin' about that doggone bridge again," complained Stretch. "Hell, kid, you're in trouble enough already. You better forget about Garvie's Gorge and think of how you're gonna out-talk a prosecution lawyer."

"Stretch, you ask too much of me," Max gently chided. "Try to understand, my friend. That dream, the vision of the bridge sagging, has come to me *several* times. A recurring

162

dream—and very clear. So it must mean *something*."

Deputy Dagget came traipsing along the corridor. Nodding nonchalantly to the Texans, he peered through the bars at the prisoner and offered a few words of comfort.

"Dunno if this'll make you feel any easier, Max. I was close by when Leroy talked to Miss Louise."

"Deputy Prowse's big moment," said Max, with a twisted grin. "I'm sure he enjoyed it."

"Maybe he did—but *she* didn't," offered Dagget. "Plain truth is the lady was weepin'."

"Miss Louise wept?" frowned Max. "For *me*?"

"I don't mean for Leroy," drawled Dagget. "He bragged of how he arrested you for the killin' of Sam Parrant and, just before she started cryin', she said as how she'd never believe it."

"A man learns who his real friends are," mused Max, "when he's up to his ears in strife —when it seems things couldn't get any worse for him."

"Well, I thought maybe you'd like to know about Miss Louise," shrugged Dagget.

163

He was turning away, when Larry thought to ask,

"Did Parrant ever get close to the B-Bar bunch?"

"Get close?" prodded Dagget.

"Was he friendly with 'em?" asked Larry. "He do any legal chores for Burchell—anything like that?"

"Nope—not that I'd know of," said Dagget. "Last time Al Burchell needed a lawyer was when the Settlers National fore-closed on a hunk of his range. He put up some of his land as—uh—what they call collateral for a loan. But, come to think of it, no lawyer could've helped Burchell out of that fix. He had time to pay, but he didn't, so the bank took over—and that was that."

"Were they acquainted?" prodded Larry. "You ever see 'em gamblin' together, maybe playin' five card stud?"

"Never did," frowned Dagget. And then, eyeing Larry intently, he asked, "You tryin' to make a point?"

"Just curious," said Larry.

The scrawny deputy eyed Larry a moment longer, then shrugged and began trudging back to the office. For a while, the drifters tried to boost Max Fitch's courage, but Larry was running short of reassuring remarks and Stretch was becoming tongue-tied. It was Max's attitude that disquieted them. Had he raged and ranted, sought solace in blistering profanity, they could have cussed along with him, on familiar ground. But he was quiet and uncomplaining, convinced that his only hope of salvation lay in his own ability to sway a jury.

"Don't worry about me," he soothed, as they made to take their leave. "I do realize the seriousness of my position, but I'll overcome it —somehow."

"You think you can dream your way out of it?" Larry challenged.

"Right here and now, you could use a vision," declared Stretch. "If you see somethin' we don't see, you better up and tell us, on account of you're gonna need all the help you can get."

Max took that advice seriously.

"If I have any premonitions, I'll let you know," he promised. "I'll have Deputy Dagget fetch you rightaway."

"Thanks a heap," said Stretch. He followed his partner back to the office, where they retrieved their weapons and nodded so-long to

Dagget and the sheriff. When they were ambling uptown toward the Heenan Hotel, he asked, "You thinkin' the lawyer could've been tied up with the B-Bar bunch?"

"So far, it's just a hunch," said Larry.

"Uh huh—and how'd you get such a hunch?" demanded Stretch.

"Kind of convenient, wasn't it?" Larry suggested. "We sashayed into the Ridley Hotel and, before we could find Parrant, there they were—Burchell's three hard case pards—crowdin' us again. Does that give you any ideas?"

"I don't catch on as fast as you," Stretch reminded him. "Go on, runt. Make it plainer."

"While we were tanglin' with Burchell's pards, some skunk was stabbin' Parrant in the back," said Larry. "The way it seems to me, it all happened about the same time. And Max's luck ran out when I sent him up to find the lawyer. He found him—sure—and then he pulled the damn-blasted knife out of Parrant's back and got himself blamed for the killin'."

"It wasn't just an unlucky accident they jumped us when they did, huh?" frowned Stretch.

"It wasn't any accident," asserted Larry.

166

"Burchell's men were buyin' some time for the killer."

"Who is likely Burchell," said Stretch.

"That's my belief," nodded Larry. "But who cares a damn what I believe? Believin' don't mean a damn unless you can back your hunches with proof."

"What the law calls evidence," mused Stretch.

"So we keep on askin' around," Larry decided. "One way or another, we have to find out if Parrant was trouble for Burchell. That lawyer wasn't knifed just for the hell of it. Somebody had a damn good reason—and I'm bettin' that 'somebody' was Burchell."

6

A FEW minutes before opening time Friday morning, Jay Taflin arrived at the Settlers National and respectfully greeted his boss, who was unlocking the street-door. There was no danger of Aaron Hinchley's observing the bulkiness of the cashier's pockets; Taflin's suit was completely shrouded by a slicker. Rain had begun falling in a thin drizzle some fifteen minutes before.

"First rain in many months," Hinchley remarked, as they entered the bank, "and it had to come today."

"The warmth of your welcome will compensate Mister Glynn for the dark clouds," Taflin predicted.

"Well said, Taflin," declared Hinchley, with a jovial smile. "And it's all arranged, I'm glad to say. An impressive reception committee, a fine representation of Logantown's civic leaders, will turn out to greet today's eastbound—rain or shine. From the depot, we'll escort Casper Glynn along Main Street to the Grand Western.

Gus Ashworth has a speech prepared, and Sheriff Waterbury is going to escort our guest with the same deference he would show President Arthur himself."

After Hinchley had disappeared into his office, Taflin transferred the balance of the counterfeit bills to his desk, completing that chore before removing his slicker. From his point of view, the rain could not have come at a better time. When he left the bank this afternoon, the counterfeit bills would remain in the vault. Their equivalent in genuine cash would be neatly packaged as well as stowed in his pockets; thanks to the all-enveloping slicker he could afford to tote a few packages, nobody would notice the bulk.

Throughout the morning and the early afternoon, the drizzle persisted, accompanied by a distant rumbling of thunder, faint at first, but becoming louder toward mid-afternoon. Larry and Stretch were out and about at this time, discussing the Parrant murder with a fine cross-section of the local citizenry, still digging, still seeking a motive that would tie Al Burchell into the case.

In his cell at the county jail, Max Fitch cat-napped, dozing fitfully and, at intervals, dreaming a bad dream. Pike Hewson stopped to visit and to report all was well at the Happy Haven Livery & Barn. Farmer Gaffney had arranged to take delivery of his mare and foal as soon as they were strong enough to be moved. In his terse, unemotional way, the stablehand assured Max of his belief in his innocence.

"Maybe you're as strange as some folks claim, young Max," he frowned, "but you're no killer."

After lunch, Webb Kilburn sauntered into the Settlers National and, on the pretext of asking to be directed to the Western Union office, had a few words in private with the cashier.

"Just in case you forgot," he warned. "I'll be outside—watching—when you close up. You know which way to head, friend. Straight to the Wheel Of Fortune—and remember I'll be tagging you close."

"I've got it all set up," Taflin softly assured him. "After Hinchley leaves, I'll start changing the fake bills for the real stuff, ought to get it done in a quarter-hour, maybe less. By closing time, I'll have it all."

"That's right," grinned Kilburn. "You'll be

a walking king's ransom when you quit the bank and head for Crane's place, so it wouldn't be smart to let you go it alone. Can't take a risk you'd have an accident, huh Taflin?"

"You'd better get out of here now," urged Taflin. "There are clients coming in."

Two hours before the eastbound rumbled across the bridge at Garvie's Gorge, the mortal remains of the venal Sam Parrant were laid to rest in the Logan County cemetery. Larry and Stretch attended the funeral and stood bareheaded, draped in their wet slickers and paying more attention to the handful of mourners than to the eulogy mumbled by the preacher, who had caught a chill and was almost inarticulate from nasal congestion. The law was not represented, Deputy Prowse having asserted that he had done his duty by the deceased by trapping and arresting his killer, Deputy Dagget being occupied with chores at the county jail, and Sheriff Waterbury being in conference with Mayor Ashworth and other members of the welcoming committee.

The drifters had hoped to find close friends of Parrant's at his funeral, intimates who might know of some connection between the lawyer and the B-Bar outfit. Larry ignored the undertaker and the grave-diggers and kept his eyes on the other people—two men and a woman—while quietly trading comments with the taller Texan.

"I still say it was too strong a coincidence—Burchell's men jumpin' us in the hotel lobby."

"And you're likely right," agreed Stretch. "If they hadn't stopped us, we'd of moseyed right up them stairs and maybe spotted the galoot that knifed Parrant."

"That's all we've got," Larry pointed out, "so we just have to keep workin' on it." Studying the woman, he asked, "You recognize her?"

"Sure. Percenter from a saloon—one of the uptown saloons, I think."

"You recollect which one?"

"Yeah, it comes back to me now. The Lucky Seven. Her name's Dolly and we already talked to her about Parrant. He was just a jasper she took a shine to."

"Now I remember her. She couldn't tell us a thing." Larry sidled closer to the undertaker and nudged him. "You know those two citizens?"

"The sawn-off is Red-Eye Barney Elliot,"

offered the undertaker. "And he sure earned his nickname."

"Barfly?"

"Sure enough—and he works hard at it. What I call a real professional."

"Close friend of Parrant's, was he?"

"Heck, no. Barney scarce knew him. Barney doesn't really know *anybody*. But he always shows up for funerals, hopin' there'll be a wake or maybe some galoot with a bottle. Shows up at weddings and christenings too—for the same reason."

"The other man looks familiar, but I can't recall where I saw him," frowned Larry.

"Nat Bischoff," said the undertaker. "If you ever had a drink at the Lucky Seven, that's where you saw him. He tends bar there."

"We must be gettin' old, runt," complained Stretch. "Imagine you and me forgettin' a barkeep!"

After the grave had been filled in and the group was dispersing, the Texans attached themselves to the bartender. They trudged through the increasing rain, bound for the heart of town, and Bischoff confided,

"I wasn't all that partial to Parrant, only

173

come to the buryin' to please Dolly. She said we had to show respect, you know?"

"You didn't much like him, but maybe you savvied him," Larry suggested. "Maybe you could tell us how Parrant stayed in business, how he operated."

"If I understand what you're gettin' at, I'd be glad to help," Bischoff assured him, "if I could."

"What we're tryin' to do is find some galoot that wanted Parrant dead," said Stretch.

"Somebody who'd profit from Parrant's dyin'," said Larry.

"Or somebody that just naturally hated his guts," said Stretch.

"He wasn't what I'd call a popular feller," shrugged the barkeep.

"No friends?" prodded Larry.

"Not that I recall."

"Well," said Stretch, "the galoot that shoved a knife in him sure wasn't no friend of his."

"Crazy Max killed Parrant," frowned Bischoff. "That's what everybody claims. And he's in jail, so I guess it's true."

"We don't see it that way," countered Larry. "We think the real killer is still on the loose."

"Holy smoke," grunted Bischoff, as the rain

174

increased, the lightning flashed and the thunder boomed.

Larry put a blunt question and struck a chord of the barkeep's memory.

"Did Parrant make any deals at the Lucky Seven? He like to talk law business over a couple shots of rye?"

"Once in a while," said Bischoff. "Come to think of it, he was in the saloon just the other day. I saw him talkin' to—let me think now—who was it?"

"You could earn yourself an easy sawbuck," declared Larry, "just by rememberin' a name."

He peeled a bill from his bankroll, crumpled it and began tossing and catching it, as they drew closer to the Lucky Seven. Bischoff, watching the green ball rise and fall, assured him,

"I'm tryin'."

"It wasn't little Max?" challenged Stretch.

"No," said Bischoff. "I hardly ever saw Fitch in the place."

"Was it a sodbuster?" prodded Larry. "A cattleman maybe?"

"*Now* I remember!" Bischoff snapped his fingers. "It was Al Burchell and his B-Bar hands. Yeah, sure. Parrant was talkin' to 'em just the other day."

"In the bar, huh?" asked Larry.

"One of the back rooms," recalled Bischoff. "Parrant didn't go right in. He was just in the doorway, talkin' soft to Burchell—so soft that I couldn't hear a word he said."

"They were talkin' sociable—or was Burchell cussin' Parrant?" demanded Larry. They had reached the batwings of the Lucky Seven. Bischoff paused, stared longingly at the $10 bill and proved himself an honest man. "I don't know what you're hopin' to hear, friend, but I ain't gonna lie. Burchell and his boys were in that rear room, but, while Parrant talked to 'em, I couldn't see their faces nor hear a word they said."

"Give him the ten," urged Stretch, and Larry gave Bischoff the ten.

The Texans walked on from the Lucky Seven in blinding rain, their ears assailed by the loudest thunder they had heard in many a long year. Raising his voice above it, Larry announced, "It ain't often I'd ask help of a lawman, but, just this once, I'm gonna break my own rule."

"Who're we gonna talk to?" asked Stretch. "The sheriff?"

"I reckon not."

"Not that pea-brained Prowse?"

"Hell, no. We'll jaw a spell with Dagget. I got a hunch he's a sight smarter than he lets on."

And so the Texans were in conference with Deputy Dagget in the law office, swigging coffee and discussing the B-Bar outfit, when the eastbound steamed into the Logantown depot. Smiling a greeting, offering their hands, Aaron Hinchley, the mayor and their cronies converged on the observation platform of the first Pullman car, as the gaunt and somewhat imperious Casper Glynn appeared. He summoned up a smile, shook Hinchley's hand and congratulated him on his record of faithful service to the company, paid his respects to Ella and Louise, and was then escorted to a waiting rig for the journey to the Grand Western Hotel.

The vehicles carrying the distinguished visitor and the reception committee rolled past the bank and into the next block, watched by Al Burchell and his three cronies from the mouth of the alley opposite. Along Main Street the lamp-lighter was at work already; dusk was a full hour away, but thickening storm clouds had spread a pall of gloom over the county, and Burchell was ready to make his move.

"It'll be full dark in a little while," he remarked. "We got everything we need, so why wait? Soon as the cashier leaves, we'll get started."

"You were gonna wait till the banquet," Thornley reminded him, "till they started on their champagne-drinkin' and their speech-makin'."

"I've changed my mind," muttered Burchell. He chuckled softly as the thunder boomed again. "Hear that?"

"You think I'm deaf?" frowned Thornley.

"It's gonna be dead easy," grinned Burchell. "When we blow the door off of that vault, who's gonna know the difference? Folks'll hear the blast, but they'll think it's thunder."

"Well, I ain't so sure," growled Cardew. "Seems to me you're takin' a lot for granted."

"If you can't use a share of what's in that vault, you can mount up and ride out," Burchell curtly invited. "You can quit right now, Cardew."

"Nobody wants to quit, Al," said Hale. "Let's get on with it."

"Soon as that cashier shuts up shop," said Burchell.

A short time later, Jay Taflin emerged from the Settlers National, shrouded by his slicker and with his hat pulled low over his face. After securing the street-door, he moved away toward the Wheel Of Fortune. And Burchell and his men, intently studying the bank, paid no attention to the second slickered figure; Webb Kilburn had emerged from the alley beside the bank and was following the cashier.

"Now we move," muttered Burchell, scanning the rain-lashed street. "Jake, you come with me. Cardew, you and Hale cross Main and half-block downtown, then make for the back alley and meet us behind the bank. It wouldn't look right, all four of us headed over there together."

Burchell and his men were leading their horses out of the alley and separating at about the same time that Jay Taflin was climbing through the window of Phil Crane's office. Kilburn came close behind him, flashing his grin at Crane, Morrison and the blonde woman.

"Anybody get curious?" challenged Morrison, as his partner closed the window. "You weren't followed?"

"Nothing to fret about," drawled Kilburn. "Main stem is damn near flooded. Not many citizens out in this rainstorm. I just picked up our boy outside the bank and tagged him all the way here. Nothing to it."

"Taflin?" prodded Crane.

"The fake stuff is packed away in the vault," Taflin reported, removing his slicker. "I left everything the way Hinchley would expect to find it on Monday morning. My guess is he won't get wise to the switch till the first client raises the alarm."

Watching Taflin dump the packages onto Crane's desk, Morrison gestured impatiently.

"Get a move on, Taflin. Let's see the whole heap. There's a train bound west out of Logantown an hour from now, and we aim to be aboard." He darted a glance at Kilburn. "You collect our tickets?"

"Couple hours ago," nodded Kilburn

"All right, Taflin, let's see the rest of it," urged Crane.

The cashier emptied his bulging pockets, trading smiles with Rose Dawes, whose eyes gleamed as she watched the green bundles piled high on the desk.

"That's all of it?" challenged Morrison.

"Every dollar," declared Taflin.

"Webb, make sure," ordered Morrison.

Taflin protested angrily, but Morrison had his way. It took Kilburn only a few moments to frisk the cashier, and then Crane and Morrison made a hasty tally of the wealth—hasty, but accurate.

"Right down the middle gents," muttered Crane, as he halved the pile. "Fifty percent, as agreed."

Kilburn scooped his and Morrison's share into the valise previously used to transport the counterfeit bills. Crane passed half of the balance to Taflin who nodded reassuringly at the frowning Rose and told her,

"I'll take care of it."

"You can trust Rose," grinned Crane. "She wouldn't run out on you." He stowed the fourth share in his safe, then produced a bottle and five glasses. "And now, let's drink to the success of our little project." Chuckling elatedly, he remarked, "There's many a bank been robbed and many a thief behind bars. But not us, my friends. We did it the *easy* way!"

"That's the way I like it," said Morrison. "No hullabaloo. No complications."

But the hullabaloo and the complications

were about to began, had Morrison but guessed it.

The back alley was deserted, when Burchell and his men re-assembled at the rear door of the Settlers National. Booming thunder muffled the sounds of splintering woodwork, as Hale attacked the door with a crowbar. Then, as Burchell and the other two hustled through the doorway, Hale discarded the crowbar and retreated to the far side of the alley; he swung astride his mount and held the reins of the other horses.

Burchell snarled an oath upon reaching the area behind the cashier's counter; he had heard the rattling sound of Cardew's matchbox.

"You show a light—I'll break every bone in your body," he threatened.

"When you set off that charge, you'll likely blow out the front windows, so what difference if I light a match now?" demanded Cardew.

"I don't want anybody sightin' a light in here before we're ready to move!" growled Burchell.

"How about the shades on those windows?" asked Thornley, glancing toward the street.

"Leave 'em down," ordered Burchell.

Working by feel, he made his way to the manager's private office and onward to the vault door. Crouching there, he dumped the sack containing his prepared explosives and went to work. Three bundles of dynamite sticks were secured to strategic sections of the door, each with a fuse some 18 inches long. Before scratching a match, he unrolled a gainsack and gestured for Thornley and Cardew to retreat to the far wall. He followed them after touching flame to the three fuses.

"Two kinds of thunder!" He had to raise his voice to make himself heard above the din of the storm, as he flopped beside Thornley. "When those charges go off, who's gonna know the difference?"

"You planned it good, Al," frowned the ramrod. "But I'll tell you somethin'. I won't feel safe till we're clear of town and back on home-range."

"Hell, Al, did you have to use so much of that stuff?" challenged Cardew.

"I savvy dynamite," Burchell curtly assured him. "You're safe enough, so long as you keep your head down and . . ."

The roar of the explosion muffled his speech. Thornley and Cardew felt a wave of hot air and began coughing frantically against the acrid stench of the blast; they were lurching to their

183

feet as Burchell stumbled away from them, steering a ragged course for the strongroom entrance. Shattered glass littered the floor under the front windows The cashier's counter was askew and the door of Hinchley's office had been blown inward. Burchell wasn't concerned with *that* door. Reaching the vault entrance, he leered triumphantly and lunged with his left shoulder. The battered wreck of the door swung inward on its one surviving hinge and, by the time his cronies joined him, Burchell was transferring the green bundles from the shelves to his sack. His voice shook, as he mumbled a command at Cardew.

"You go check the alley. We'll be right out." He slid another four bundles from a shelf and into the bag, and told Thornley, "Watch the street."

Gingerly, Thornley approached the front wall. Glass crackled under his feet, as he darted a glance along the lamp-lit, rain-lashed thoroughfare.

"See anybody?" demanded Burchell.

"Not many people about," said Thornley. "Nobody lookin' this way." He winced and clapped hands to his ears as the thunder boomed again. "Hell's bells" Damn storm feels like it'll *never* quit!"

"Don't gripe, Jake," chuckled Burchell. "It's gonna make our chore that much easier." He made a quick check of the shelves, ignoring the sacks of coins, reaching for a sheaf of documents, then tossing them aside. "I reckon that's it. We got a fortune right here in this ol' sack —enough for all of us." Having secured the neck of the sack with a length of twine, he slung it over his shoulder. "All right—we're movin' out."

Thornley followed him along the passage to the rear door, where Cardew awaited them, crooking a finger and announcing,

"We got the whole alley to ourselves."

"Won't take no chances anyway," Burchell decided, as he led them across to the horses. "We'll turn left at the next corner. That'll take us across the vacant lot and into Wicker's Road. "We're quittin' town by the east side?" demanded Thornley, raising a boot to stirrup.

"That's the fastest way out," Burchell reminded him. He secured the neck of the sack to his saddlehorn and swung astride. "First we get clear of town. Then we can take our time swingin' north to the old McGowan trail." As they nudged their mounts to movement, he called a final warning. "Just move along steady. If we try to hustle these animals in this damn storm, some nosy citizen might sight us—and remember."

For three whole minutes it seemed their departure would be orderly, unmarred by violent incident. They advanced along the back alley toward the corner, their horses plodding cautiously through the mud and slush, the rain bouncing off their sodden Stetsons and gleaming slickers. Then came the unexpected.

Abruptly, the rain stopped falling, the thunder ceased as suddenly as an interrupted drum-roll, so that the sound of hooves plodding through mud seemed uncommonly loud.

Just as abruptly, two familiar figures appeared, emerging from a doorway to their right. Larry and Stretch—forever restless—had parted company with Deputy Dagget a short time before and returned to their room at the Heenan Hotel. Stretch had then decided that Dagget's coffee had given him a thirst for cold beer, so now they were on the move again, quitting the hotel and thinking of collecting the convivial Doc Milford en route to the nearest saloon. But one of the four horsemen changed their minds.

Had Cardew not lost his head, the Texans might never have noticed the riders. They were turning toward Main Street, when the ugly hard case recognized them and reacted quickly, rashly. Burchell gasped a warning, but too late. Cardew had emptied his holster and opened fire, and the Texans were cursing lustily, whirling and delving under their slickers for the butts of their Colts.

"*Move*—you damn idiot!" raged Burchell. "Let up on that shootin' . . . !"

Larry's gun was half-drawn and he was side-stepping toward the nearest cover, a rain-barrel, when his feet slipped in the mud. He fell, cursing luridly, and Stretch flopped to one knee beside him, aimed in the general direction of Cardew's gun-flash and squeezed trigger. Under those conditions, accurate shooting was well nigh impossible; the rain had stopped, but there was little visiblity, because this section of the alley was a fair distance from the nearest street-lamp. Cardew snarled an oath and cut loose again and it was Stretch's turn to drop flat. He ducked in urgent haste, as the bullet nicked an inch from the brim of his Stetson. Flopping beside Larry, half of his face shoved into mud, he complained,

"Everybody takes a shot at us! What'd we do? What are we anyway? They declared open season on Texans in this here territory?"

Larry didn't answer. He was struggling to his knees, spitting mud and trying to focus on the opposition. The four riders were invisible now. He heard the receding thud of hooves and took solace from the thought that, wherever they were headed, they could not afford to hustle; the condition of the ground—slushy and slippery—made fast riding risky.

"Why . . . ?" Stretch began again.

"How the hell would I know?" scowled Larry, as they lurched to their feet. "Hey—did you get a look at 'em?"

"I can't see in the dark," growled Stretch. "Neither could they—and that was lucky for us. If they'd seen us clearer, we'd be dead Texans now."

"I think they did see us," frowned Larry. "At least long enough to recognize us."

"How could they . . . ?"

"When we stepped out of that doorway—just before we shut the door. There was a light in the passage."

"Well, maybe they knew who they were shootin' at, but that don't tell us *why*."

"They came from down the alley a ways," recalled Larry.

About to sheathe his Colt, he tensed to the sound of boots slogging through mud. A figure materialized, advancing from the street-end of the side alley.

"Who's there?" challenged Davey Dagget. "Name yourselves!"

"It's us, Davey," Larry said impatiently. "Tag along."

"Tag along where?" demanded the deputy, as he fell in beside them. "Didn't I hear shootin' a couple minutes ago? Maybe I'm gettin' old, but I can still tell the difference 'tween thunder and a gunshot."

"They cut loose at us right after the thunder stopped," Larry told him. "Four riders . . ."

"We didn't get a clear look at 'em and we don't know why they threw down on us," said Larry, anticipating Dagget's next question.

"They rode thataway," offered Stretch. He jerked a thumb. "Slow and cautious. Any fool tries to run a horse through mud, he's just beggin' for a broken neck."

"Where are *you* headed?" Dagget demanded,

cursing as he almost slipped in his haste to keep pace with Larry.

"I was born curious," said Larry. "Somebody takes a shot at me, I have to know why. So I'm back-trackin' 'em—in case they . . ."

"Holy sufferin' Hannah!" breathed Stretch. "Will you look at that?"

"It ain't the first busted door I ever saw," declared Dagget, after loosing another curse. "But this one is more important than most."

"On account of . . . ?" challenged Larry.

"It happens to be the rear door of the Settlers National Bank," scowled the deputy, "or all that's left of it."

He stumbled over the fallen door and, tagged by the Texans, moved along the corridor to the front of the bank. Stretch scratched a match and observed several lamps, all of them useless, their funnels shattered by the explosion. Dagget, after a cursory inspection of the strongroom entrance, shrugged philosophically and remarked,

"It had to happen sooner or later. The only Logantown bank that's never been robbed—and now it happens—right when Aaron Hinchley's gettin' congratulated by his big boss."

190

"Congratulated for what?" asked Stretch.

"He's managed banks for the Settlers National company for better than fifteen years," said Dagget, moving toward the street-door. "No bank of his was ever robbed before."

"Somebody," Larry observed, "is makin' up for lost time."

Dagget wasn't surprised to find that the street-door could be opened without benefit of a key. The force of the blast had torn the hinges away from timber and plaster; at his touch, the door clattered outward.

"I got to find Todd Waterbury and get a posse organized," he announced. "You two want to ride with us?"

"The posse can try followin' us," countered Larry, as he tagged Dagget out to the sidewalk. "We'll be saddled up and trailin' those riders by the time your volunteers have found their guns."

Dagget called no protest when the Texans ran along the sidewalk toward the Colley Road corner; the next few hours could be hectic, and he wasn't about to waste his breath. At the law office, he broke the big news to Leroy Prowse and cut short his shocked reaction with a suggestion he start rounding up volunteers for a posse.

"You can call in Dan Wilson to guard Fitch while we're gone," he added.

"Waterbury better be told," frowned Prowse, donning his slicker.

"That'll be my chore," said Dagget. "He's up to the Grand Western with Aaron Hinchley and the mayor and that big shot from Seattle—boss of the whole Settlers National chain."

"You tell Louise's father I'm on the job," urged Prowse. "That'll comfort him."

"I'll bet," grunted Dagget.

Larry and Stretch got their first break a few minutes after clearing Logantown's outskirts, at which time Deputy Dagget was trucking mud into the expensively-carpeted lobby of the town's most exclusive hotel. Pausing where the regular stage route began, cocking their ears to the night sounds, the Texans heard the tail-end of a shouted oath somewhere ahead. The sound was far-off, barely audible, but their keen ears caught it.

"Don't have to be the jaspers we're after," Stretch warned, as they nudged their mounts to movement.

"Don't have to be," agreed Larry. "But we'll take a look anyway."

"Take a look he says! Who can see in this dark?"

"It'll be lighter soon."

"What makes you so sure about that?"

"Take a look. The storm blew itself out. Sky's clearing. Soon as those clouds roll away from the moon . . ."

"All right, we'll have moonlight," Stretch conceded. "But that don't mean we could pick up their tracks."

"Let's find out who hollered," said Larry.

In the brushy quarter-mile between the stage route and the old McGowan Road, one of the bank-robbers had come to grief; Thornley's mount had slipped and fallen into a patch of deep, glutinous mud. They were dragging the animal to harder ground and cursing impatiently, ignoring Burchell's demand for quiet, when the Texans began their advance.

"You want the whole damn territory to hear?" scowled Burchell, as the startled horse neighed in alarm. "Keep that critter *quiet*!"

"What the hell, Al?" challenged Hale. "A scared critter always hollers."

"He's clear!" panted Thornley. "Steady, boy.

193

Stead-eee . . ." He fitted a boot to stirrup, remounted and warily walked the panting pony clear of the mud-patch. "All right, Al, we better keep movin'."

"That's fine by me!" snarled Burchell. "Just so long as that fool animal of yours don't step in no more holes!" He was about to wheel his mount and press on toward the forgotten McGowan Road, when his hypersensitive ears detected the sounds of pursuit. He muttered a command. Thornley and the other two drew rein. "Listen!"

"What . . . ?" began Cardew.

"Could've sworn I heard horses." Burchell pointed westward. "Comin' from town."

"So damn *soon*?" frowned Thornley. "Hell!"

The sounds were not repeated; Larry had called a halt at the summit of a timbered rise. From there, the Texans were scanning the terrain to the east. They too were listening. On ground softened by heavy rain, the hooves of horses made little sound to be detected by a pursuer, but, sooner or later, a shod hoof might strike rock—and *that* sound would carry.

"You're gettin' jumpy, Al," chided Hale. "I don't hear a damn thing."

"We'll keep movin'," muttered Burchell.

"The sooner we're cachin' this sack at B-Bar, the easier I'll feel."

In Logantown, the news was spreading fast. Deputy Prowse, accosting townmen in the saloons and urging them volunteer for the posse, added a prediction calculated to boost his chances of becoming the county's next sheriff. He would, he loudly declared, pursue them to the mountains or all the way to the Colorado border if needs be. Pursue who? Why, the thieves who broke into the Settlers National, dynamited the vault and made off with all the paper-money—who else?

Casper Glynn, president of the Settlers National Banking Company, was entertaining his well-wishers in his suite at the Grand Western—a few appetizers before descending to the dining room for the banquet organized in his honor—when Davey Dagget intruded. The scrawny lawman was apologetic, but as blunt as ever; he was a spade-caller from way back. Todd Waterbury discarded a half-finished drink. The mayor swore explosively and flopped into a chair. Aaron Hinchley blinked incredulously and the guest of honor turned beetroot-red, as Dagget said his piece.

"Sure am sorry to bust in on you gents, but

it just can't be helped. Todd, you ain't gonna
have time for no fancy supper. Bunch of hard
cases emptied the strongroom at the bank." He
added, nodding respectfully to Hinchley. "Your
bank."

"No . . . !" gasped Hinchley.

"How many?" demanded Waterbury, on his
way to the door.

"Larry Valentine figures four at least," said
Dagget. "Him and Emerson were comin' out
the rear door of the Heenan Hotel just as a
bunch of riders come past. They got shot at.
Seems like these bandidos is trigger-happy."

"Our vault has a combination lock!"
protested Hinchley.

"They didn't unlock that door natural,
Mister Hinchley," drawled the deputy. "Plain
truth is the bank locks—uh—kind of toilworn
right now. They done blasted that door off."

"Blasted it?" gasped Hinchley.

"I presume he means with dynamite,"
frowned Casper Glynn. Shaking his head sadly,
he opined, "Logantown is no better than any
other cattle community. No bank is safe. Yours
was a fine record, Hinchley, but . . ."

"I assure you, Mister Glynn . . ." began
Hinchley.

"Got to ask you gents to excuse me," said Waterbury. "I got chores."

He hurried from the suite with Dagget in tow, while Mayor Ashworth poured a stiff shot of brandy for Hinchley and placed it in his trembling hand. Hinchley took a pull at it, stared aghast at Casper Glynn and tried again.

"I assure you—this is unprecedented. As manager of the Logantown branch, I've adhered strictly to every rule laid down by you and the board. All precautions are observed . . ."

"Hinchley, I don't doubt your efficiency nor your loyalty to the company," Glynn gruffly assured him. "However—under the circumstances—we'd best call off the celebration. Logantown has a newspaper, does it not? Of course. And what of the company's reputation? Our prestige will suffer a crippling blow, when people read of a successful robbery of the Logantown branch—perpetrated while the civic leaders were playing host to the president of the company."

"I'll vouch for the discretion of Editor Stockton," Ashworth quickly offered. "Damn him—I'll *muzzle* him if I must!"

"Freedom of the press, Mister Mayor," shrugged Glynn. "Not only is he entitled to

197

report the robbery. He could wire the story to all the big dailies back east and along the west coast." Grim-faced, he added, "Including Seattle."

"Todd Waterbury is an expert man-hunter," asserted Ashworth, conveniently forgetting that the Logan County sheriff hadn't investigated a bank robbery in better than eight years. "I believe I can guarantee prompt action, a speedy and successful conclusion to Todd's investigations."

"Let's be realistic, my friends," said Glynn. "My wisest course would be to leave Logantown—quietly—and as soon as possible."

"If you'd just reconsider . . ." began Hinchley.

"Is there a westbound passing through tonight?" demanded Glynn.

The mayor sighed heavily, consulted his watch and nodded.

"In less than an hour, Mister Glynn."

"You'll oblige me by arranging my passage," said Glynn. "Hinchley, the deputy reported the vault had been emptied. If they used dynamite to wreck the door, we must assume your ledgers and files have suffered serious damage. So—there'll be no time for a banquet."

"I'll have to—get along to the bank right-away—and check the damage." Hinchley nodded slowly, trudged to the door, then paused to offer a last apology. "I feel—as though the ground were falling away from under me. What can I say, Mister Glynn? I've been proud of my record—maybe *too* proud . . ."

"Having adhered to all the company rules, you have no cause to reproach yourself," said Glynn.

"That," countered Hinchley, "doesn't make me feel any easier."

Bart Morrison and Webb Kilburn were relaxing in Phil Crane's office, drinking to the success of their nefarious enterprise, when Rose Dawes rapped at the door and identified herself. Crane unlocked the door and admitted her, puzzled by her tense expression. He was about to close the door when Jay Taflin appeared. The cashier was looking just as apprehensive as the blonde woman.

As Crane re-secured the door, Morrison eyed Taflin coldly and declared,

"If this galoot is back to ask for a fatter share of the loot, I'll fix him so his own mother wouldn't recognize him."

"Morrison, I'm just hoping I'll get to *spend* my share," Taflin retorted. "Haven't you heard the news?"

"What news?" demanded Crane.

Rose Dawes began explaining the changed situation while pouring herself a drink. She needed a boost for her nerves.

7

MORRISON and his partner listened, but without looking at the blonde woman. They had retreated to the open window and were noting the new activity, locals hustling in and out of the nearby alleys, gathering on street-corners to swap opinions about the bank robbery, converging on the area in front of the Settlers National to gape at the shattered windows and sagging door.

When she had told all she knew, Morrison drawled a comment.

"One hell of a coincidence, but no skin off our noses."

"Coincidence is right," grinned Kilburn. "By Judas, I'd like to see their faces when they start divvying up their loot."

"Maybe the posse will run 'em down," said Morrison. "Then again, maybe they'll make a clean getaway. I don't much care—either way. We'll be gone from Logantown pretty soon, headed west on that Idaho-bound train."

"So you feel safe—but what about us?"

challenged Taflin. He sidled closer to Rose and slid an arm about her waist. "Rose and me were gonna make our move tomorrow, quitting the territory in a rented buggy . . ."

"Sure." Morrison nodded impatiently. "Going on a little picnic."

"I daren't wait that long—not now," fretted Taflin. "What happens if the sheriff catches up with those thieves tonight? Hinchley would check the recovered loot and, rightaway, he'd get wise. I'd be in a spot, Morrison."

"You got paid off," shrugged Morrison. "Make your own arrangements." He nudged Kilburn and made for the door. "Thanks for the hospitality, Crane."

"My pleasure," frowned the saloonkeeper.

"We'll get packed and head on down to the depot," Morrison told him.

"Listen, couldn't we all quit town on that westbound train?" suggested Taflin. "Logantown won't be safe for any of us . . . !"

"Take it easy, Jay honey," murmured Rose.

"You make your own arrangements," Morrison said coldly. "I never was partial to a fool that turns yellow when the chips are down. Taflin, heed what I'm telling you. Stay clear of Webb and me from here on."

"You were useful, Taflin," conceded Kilburn, "but now our little deal is finished—all debts paid. We go our way. You go yours."

"Which means," said Morrison, "stay off that train."

He nodded curtly to Crane and the woman and strode from the office, followed by Kilburn. For a brief moment, Rose matched stares with the saloonkeeper, her expression challenging, warning. He nodded reassuringly, not for Taflin's benefit; for hers.

"You got nothing to worry about," he muttered. I'll see you safe to the Idaho border, Jay. I guess I owe you that much."

"Damn right you owe me," declared Taflin. "Without me, you couldn't have swung this deal. I was the key-man, wasn't I?"

"You sure were," nodded Crane. "And the least I can do is get you out of the county." He patted the cashier's shoulder, gave him a cigar and a light. "More than that, I'll drive you across the mountains and the Idaho line. You ever hear of Byrne Junction, Taflin? Just across the border. It's a relay station for the Houghton Stage Line. From there, you and Rose could ride a coach all the way to Oregon. I'd say that's the fastest way you could quit Logan County."

"You'd drive us?" asked Taflin.

"I own the handsomest, strongest surrey in the county," bragged Crane, "and a pair of bays that would never fail us along that mountain route. If you and Rose don't mind travelling light, just one bag each . . ."

"Rose . . . ?" frowned Taflin.

"It's the best offer we're apt to get," she shrugged.

"Be ready in fifteen minutes," urged Crane, consulting his watch. "I'll arrange for Jerry and Steve to keep an eye on things while I'm gone. We could be across Garvie's Gorge by midnight and well on our way to the western foothills by dawn."

"Go pack your bag," said Rose. "I'll be ready by the time you get back." She waited for the cashier to quit the room, then stared hard at Crane and said, bitterly, "I smell a double-cross."

"What do you care?" he challenged. "I mean —so long as *you* aren't double-crossed?"

"It better not be me," she warned.

"Listen, I couldn't talk freely in front of the others," said Crane. "With you I'll be frank, sweetheart. If the posse finds those bank robbers—and the fake greenbacks—you and I

204

will be in as much grief as Taflin. It wouldn't take Hinchley long to realize the switch had been made by his own cashier. Taflin's the only other man knew the combination to the vault."

"So Hinchley runs to the sheriff . . ." she frowned.

"And Waterbury starts back-tracking Taflin's movements over the past few days," nodded Crane. "Figure it out for yourself, Rose. Every towner who drinks or gambles in the Wheel of Fortune knows Taflin was courting you."

"Waterbury would start adding two and two," she murmured.

"No lawman could faze you—but can we say the same for Taflin?" drawled Crane. "If he found himself in a cell, he'd panic and talk his fool head off. He'd name us all." He glanced at his safe, grinned sardonically and opined, "This would be a fine time—the ideal time—for me to disappear from Logan County."

"Go—and never come back? Leave it all behind?"

"Leave *what* behind? The saloon? I can always build another Wheel of Fortune—so long as I'm free and solvent. We'll take it all, Rose. Every dollar from my safe, yours and

Taflin's share—all of it—and start fresh somewhere on the west coast."

"And what happens to Taflin?"

"I'll take care of him after we've crossed the gorge. Somewhere high in the mountains, Rose. Some lonely place where he'll never be found." Crane grinned blandly. "And then we keep on rolling—just the two of us—the way you always wanted."

She went to him, linked her arms about his neck and pressed her mouth to his, and murmured, "I'll be changing to a travelling outfit, while you're fetching the rig."

All interested parties were on the move during the next 45 minutes. Crane, Taflin and the blonde woman left town quietly and took to the mountain trail, while Morrison and Kilburn squatted by their baggage in the office of the railroad depot and awaited the westbound. The counterfeiters were presently joined by a few more westbound passengers, one of whom was Casper Glynn, escorted by a woebegone Aaron Hinchley.

Fifteen townmen had volunteered to ride with Waterbury and his deputies. They rode as fast as the prevailing conditions would permit, after quitting Logantown and making for the regular route north. Because the Texans had traded shots with the thieves at a point north of the Settlers National, it never occurred to Waterbury that they might have circled the township and travelled south. For once in his life, the veteran badge-toter was jumping to conclusions, but, as subsequent events proved, he could afford to do so.

Leroy Prowse was very much to the fore, riding slightly ahead of his chief and frequently turning to beckon the volunteers, a gesture that caused Waterbury and Dagget some amusement.

"Why does he keep wavin' us on?" grinned Dagget.

"Who cares?" shrugged the sheriff. "As long as it keeps him happy . . ."

A short distance along the stage route, a halt was called and the surface of the trail checked by lamp-light. There was moonlight, but not enough of it to permit the reading of sign. Grim-faced, but clinging to his patience, Waterbury stayed mounted and lit a cigar. Prowse, accompanied by a barkeep, a blacksmith and a couple of bookkeepers, made quite a ceremony of studying the soggy ground and announcing his findings. The barkeep disagreed and so did one of the bookkeepers and, when the argument became noisy and heated, Waterbury grimaced in disgust and growled a reproach.

"This back-talk is gettin' us nowhere. Say it plain, Leroy, for pity's sakes. Have you cut their sign, or haven't you?"

"I claim they're staying on the regular stage route," said Prowse. "That proves they're strangers. They don't dare quit the marked trail for fear they'd get lost." He tensed and dropped a hand to his holster, twisting to stare eastward. "Careful, men! Somebody coming!"

"Uh huh, sure," grunted Dagget. "But, listen Leroy, I wouldn't start shootin' rightaway if I was you. Ain't no hostile Sioux this far south . . ."

Some of the possemen began laughing. Prowse colored and cursed, while Waterbury turned in his saddle and watched the two riders. They advanced close enough to be recognized, traded nods with the lawmen and said their piece.

"Must be some kind of trail over thataway," drawled Larry, gesturing to the northeast. "We heard riders a little while back, and . . ."

"That's impossible," snapped Prowse.

"There's no trail in that direction, no route a horse could travel—specially in all this mud."

"Nothin' but the old McGowan road," frowned Dagget.

"They couldn't ride *that* old trail," argued Waterbury. "No man could."

"Hasn't been used in years," Dagget explained to the Texans. "You know what happens to a path cut through brush and timber when nobody uses it any more. It grows over again."

"Are we gonna waste time talking about the old McGowan trail?" demanded Prowse. "While we dilly dally, those thieving coyotes are getting clear away, making the miles!"

"We ain't dillyin', Leroy," chided Waterbury.

"Nor dallyin'," drawled Dagget.

"Horses needed spellin' anyway," Waterbury pointed out. "A winded horse won't tote you far on a night like this." He raised his eyes to the sky, then scanned the moonlit terrain ahead. "Thanks for the information, you two," he nodded to the Texans. "Maybe the riders you heard are the same bunch we're after, but the wind plays strange tricks. You couldn't have

209

heard 'em that far northeast of this trail. More likely they were dead ahead."

"That's what I keep trying to tell you!" shouted Prowse.

"No need to holler, Leroy," frowned Waterbury. "I ain't deaf." He nodded to the Texans again. "Welcome to ride along with us, if you got a mind to."

"Tell you what, Sheriff," said Stretch. "Just in case we were right—I mean about where them riders was headed . . ."

"Just in case," finished Larry, "we'll go find this old trail you talked of."

"You'll need a guide," said Dagget. "A stranger could never find his way." Glancing at his chief, he suggested, "Might be there's somethin' to what Valentine says so one of us ought to tag along with 'em."

"You volunteerin'?" asked the sheriff.

"Wild goose chase," jeered Prowse.

That decided Dagget.

"You got more men than you can use anyway," he reminded his chief.

"If you want to ride along with Valentine and Emerson, it's all right by me," said Waterbury. He grinned wryly and reflected, "The joke'd be on us, if those thieves found their way to the McGowan route and got lost."

"How much longer are we gonna . . . ?" began Prowse.

"By golly, Leroy, you'll be the noisiest sheriff this county ever had—if you do get elected," sighed Waterbury. "All right, men, let's keep movin'. Watch yourself, Davey. I'll be seein' you."

"Likewise," nodded Dagget.

Unhurriedly, he ambled his mount off the trail and across to where the Texans waited. They watched Waterbury and his volunteers move off behind Prowse, who had remounted quickly and was pointing northward, as though the posse had forgotten the direction.

"That Prowse . . ." Larry grinned derisively.

"He's happy, I guess," shrugged Stretch. "Couldn't be any happier if he had a brain in his head."

"If he gets to be sheriff, I'll quit totin' a badge and take to outlawry," Dagget decided. "While ever he's in charge of law and order, I reckon I could get away with *anything*." He glanced northeast and asked, "You sure of what you heard?"

"Could be the same bunch tried to gun us

down in town," opined Larry. "We heard 'em cussin'."

"And, a little while later, we found the place where a horse got stuck in the mud," offered Stretch.

"How in blazes could you read sign at night?" challenged Dagget. "I'll allow there's moonlight, but it ain't all that bright."

"We took a chance, lit a few matches," said Stretch.

"Four horses," Larry said bluntly. "Headed northeast—nothin' surer. I didn't hanker to argue it with the sheriff, specially while that bonehead Prowse was throwin' in his ten cents worth."

"Davey, what's northeast anyway?" asked Stretch.

"Open range and a cattle spread or two," said Dagget. "McCormack's Double Seven, the Lazy J and B-Bar, the Burchell outfit . . ."

"One way or another, we keep runnin' into Burchell and his pards," Stretch remarked.

"Yeah." Larry nodded slowly. "One way or another."

They turned their mounts and rode to right and left of Dagget, as he started across the open ground to the spot where a B-Bar horse had been temporarily bogged down. From their, they travelled faster; avoiding the soft stretches was easier, now that they had acquired a guide. In little more than twenty minutes, the deputy was leading them into what looked to be an impenetrable tangle of brush, and the horses balked until Stretch scratched a match. In the split second before the wind killed the flame, Larry glimpsed the opening. Dagget cursed softly and dropped to the ground; it was his turn to scratch a match or two.

Standing beside Larry's horse, he inspected a broken sprig of juniper.

"Fresh," he declared. "As fresh as the hoofmarks."

"So the idea ain't so crazy," muttered Larry.

"Somebody's travellin' a trail that ain't been used in many a long year," growled Dagget. "Would a stranger find this route—at night? The hell he would!"

"More likely they're local men," said Larry.

"Couldn't get rich by honest toil," musted Stretch, "so they did a little night-time chore —with dynamite."

"Let's hope they used *all* their dynamite to bust that vault door," said Larry.

"I reckon I follow your meanin', friend," said

Dagget. "We wouldn't look so purty if they sighted us and flung just one stick—with a short fuse."

"You scared already?" prodded Stretch.

"I'll tell you when I'm scared," growled Dagget. "Let's go."

They moved onto the southern section of the old trail in Indian file, Dagget leading, Larry following and Stretch bringing up the rear. And, though it wound tortuously, they travelled at a steady clip, making good time. The way had been blazed for them by the four riders who had plowed through a short time before; their markers were the jagged, broken saplings and torn brush at either side.

It took them almost a half-hour to reach the northern reaches of the old trail, and then they were moving across open ground in bright moonlight. Instinctively, the Texans widened the gap separating them from Dagget and dropped their right hands to their holsters. Travelling the old trail, they had been sheltered, their movements concealed. Now they were wide open, vulnerable, and conscious of it.

"That rock-wall dead ahead . . ." Larry

called softly to the deputy. "Is there a way through, or do we have to ride around it?"

"We'd lose a lot of time ridin' around it," muttered Dagget. "There's a cleft leads straight through, kind of like a saber cut, you know? Coffin Canyon it's called."

"Sounds plumb cheerful," mumbled Stretch. "And what's yonder?"

"Yonder is the south quarter of B-Bar," frowned the deputy.

"It gets interestin', don't it?" remarked Stretch.

"It sure as hell do," nodded Dagget.

Okay now, when we reach the south end of the canyon, we're gonna check for their sign again," Larry decided.

"Yeah, we'll check," agreed Dagget, "and likely find it." As they advanced warily on the opening in the rock-wall, he asked, "Don't neither of you jaspers want to know why it's called Coffin Canyon?" The Texans shook their heads. Dagget grimaced impatiently. "It's on account of it's shaped like a doggone coffin."

"We'll take your word for that," shrugged Larry.

"Just a little bitty cut at the north and south ends," said Dagget. "There ain't no other way

215

in nor out. Canyon walls are steep—too steep for . . ."

"Hold it," frowned Larry. He manoeuvered his mount closer to the deputy's and dropped his voice to a whisper. "Keep your voice down."

"I don't hear . . ." began Dagget.

"Well, *I* do." They had reached the opening, and now Larry was hearing the echoing voices inside the canyon, voices raised in strident profanity. "You deaf all of a sudden?"

"I hear 'em," breathed Dagget, drawing his six-gun.

"You suppose they've spotted us?" demanded Sretch.

"That ain't why they're cussin'," opined Larry.

"Watch yourself," warned Dagget, as Larry nudged the sorrel forward. "Once you're through the cleft, they'll see you clear. There's no cover inside."

"Which means I'll see them just as clear," Larry retorted.

Stretch and the deputy tagged him through the opening, then wheeled to right and left of him, their guns out and cocked, their eyes on the four horsemen at the north end of the high-walled corridor. Larry, studying the riders, noted the sack slung from Burchell's saddle-horn. The B-Bar men were unaware of the new arrivals; all their attention was focussed on the end of the canyon.

"Where's the north gate?" Larry called to Dagget.

"It's filled in, damnitall!" growled Dagget. "The storm must've started an avalanche. By Judas, they rode into a trap! We got 'em boxed!"

At the north end of the canyon, Al Burchell glowered at the heap of rock and rubble blocking what had once been a natural outlet; he gave vent to one last blistering oath, then declared,

"We got nothin' to win by tryin' to clear it. Too big a chore for us."

"It'd take hours—and a lot of muscle," complained Thornley.

"Too bad you used all that dynamite," muttered Cardew.

"Just a few sticks'd do it."

"No use hangin' around here, cussin' and gettin' noplace," shrugged Burchell.

"Let's move out," urged Thornley, wheeling his mount. "I don't relish the idea of gettin'

217

stuck in this damn bottleneck. If the posse . . ."

"Posse ain't had time to get here," said Burchell. "We had too long a start on 'em."

"*Somebody* had time!" gasped Hale, emptying his holster. "Look there!"

Burchell swore luridly and jerked back on his rein. Hefting his Colt, he watched the three riders begin their slow, determined advance from the south end of the canyon. And then, as they drew closer, he recognized them.

"It's Dagget—and them Texas saddle-tramps!"

The snarled announcement carried clear to the deputy, who quietly remarked, "It's B-Bar. Al Burchell and his proddy sidekicks. I might've guessed."

"Maybe they're just out for a moonlight ride," drawled Larry.

"Oh, sure," grinned Stretch. "And they started their ride in the alley back of the bank."

"Sack hung from Burchell's saddle," observed Larry. "I got twenty dollars says that sack is full of greenbacks."

"No bet," grunted Dagget. They advanced another fifteen yards, while Burchell and his men spread themselves, Cardew and Hale

218

hustling their mounts toward the west wall, the rogue rancher and his ramrod edging to the east side. Dagget rose in his stirrups to hurl his challenge and, automatically, the Texans readied themselves for a shooting showdown. Larry slid his Winchester from its sheath, cocked it and nudged the stock into his left shoulder while hefting his Colt in his right fist. Stretch emptied his leftside holster; with his matched .45's he was ambidexterous. "Burchell! Al Burchell . . . !"

"You want somethin', Deputy?" challenged Burchell.

"Depends!" yelled Dagget.

"Depends on *what*?"

"Whats in the sack, Burchell?" You want to tell me—or do I come take a look?"

"Try it and you're dead!" raged Burchell.

"Easy, Al," frowned Thornley. "They're between us and the only way out. Better you should try a bluff . . ."

"I'm through talkin'!" Burchell was tremblin' in fury and frustration, incensed by the sight of three riders blocking his escape route. He leaned forward, touched the bulging sack and swore an oath. "Any tin star, any saddlebum takes this dinero, it has to be over my dead body."

"Burchell!" called Dagget. "I'm accusin' you of robbin' the Settlers National! If I'm wrong, you can sue me! Meantime—I want to see what's in that sack!"

"Cardew—Hale . . . !" bellowed Burchell. "Let 'em have it!"

He fired, thumbed back his hammer and fired again, then started his mount bounding along the base of the east wall. Thornley followed, shooting fast but wildly at Dagget and the Texans. The deputy toppled from his mount during that first rapid exchange, not because he was critically wounded, but for the sake of drawing a clear bead on the fast-moving riders from a prone position; Burchell's bullet had scored a shallow crease along his left forearm. Sprawled on his belly, he extended his right arm, took careful aim and fired and saw Thornley back-somersault from his pony.

Cardew was rashly charging Larry, who had reined up and was more than ready for him. A bullet whined past his face as he steadied his Winchester and squeezed trigger, and that was the only shot fired by Cardew. He pitched from his mount, while Hale yelled a challenge, his voice rising above the thunder of his Colt.

"He's yours, runt!" called Stretch, as he wheeled his mount. "I'm after Burchell! If he gets past Davey . . . !"

"Get goin'," urged Larry.

He hunched his shoulders and growled an oath. One of Hale's fast-triggered slugs had missed his right shoulder with only inches to spare. Another won a startled whinny from the sorrel when it seared the top of the saddlehorn. Hale didn't rate a third chance, to Larry's way of thinking. He drew a fast bead and cut loose with his .45 and, for the second time in less than a minute, emptied a saddle. Hale went to ground in an untidy, lifeless heap, and then Larry was wheeling his mount and staring away to the right and to his rear, checking on Dagget and the taller Texan.

Dagget had stopped firing. He was rising to his knees, fumbling with his pistol and cursing bitterly and, had Stretch's pinto not moved so swiftly, Burchell might have made it to the canyon's southern outlet. The rancher was twisting in his saddle, his six-shooter swinging toward Stretch at deadly short range, when Stretch's righthand Colt boomed. Burchell yelled, but the yell was cut short when, knocked off-balance by the impact of the bullet, he pitched from his speeding pony and struck the canyon-wall head-first.

"Stay after his damn-blasted horse!" roared Dagget. "I'll swear that cayuse is totin' a fortune!"

Stretch caught up with the riderless animal a few yards from the canyon entrance, holstered both pistols and reached over to grasp its bridle. The pony baulked a moment, then turned obediently, demoralized by his full-throated profanity. He started back toward the center of the canyon-floor, where Dagget still fiddled with his .45. Larry was advancing from the west side and leading two horses, one toting the wounded and unconscious Cardew, the other carrying Hale's body. As they reached the deputy, he spat in disgust and returned his Colt to its holster.

"Damn iron jammed," he complained, "right when I had a bead on Burchell."

"It happens," shrugged Larry. He glanced to right and left and observed, "No wood for a fire. It wouldn't be dry enough anyway." He watched Stretch dismount and unsling the sack.

"You two can check on the dinero while I fetch Burchell and the other one."

"When I gunned Thornley, the ramrod, I didn't shoot to kill," offered Dagget.

"Bueno," grunted Larry. "He'll do then."

"Do for what?" demanded Dagget.

"I don't believe that was coincidence—Burchell's men jumpin' us in the hotel lobby," drawled Larry. "I still claim they were tryin' to keep us busy. They had somethin' to hide."

"Listen now, Larry, if you're gonna try fazin' Thornley—and him a wounded prisoner—I don't want to know about it," said Dagget. "I guess I'll have to turn my back."

"Turn your back be damned," growled Larry. "Come and watch—and listen."

Stretch had unfastened the sack and was studying the contents by matchlight.

"Mucho dinero," he wistfully announced. "So help me Hannah, it looks like all the money in the world."

"Hang it on my saddle," ordered Dagget, as he started after Larry.

Burchell's neck was broken. He lay by the rock-wall at the east-side, twisted grotesquely, his sightless eyes turned up to the night sky. They left him and moved on to where Thornley lay, arriving just as the ramrod struggled to a sitting position. Haggard and trembling, bedeviled by pain from his bullet-gashed shoulder, he was incapable of retrieving his fallen pistol. Larry picked up the weapon, handed it to Dagget, then coolly informed Thornley.

"We know the truth about the Parrant killing now. Your boss told us—just before he cashed in. I guess, at the end, he wanted to wipe his slate clean."

"I don't care," groaned Thornley. "I don't —care a damn—about *anything*. This slug is gonna kill me—I *know* it . . . !"

"There's no slug in you," muttered Dagget, examining the wound. "I nicked you, Thornley, but deep. You'll heal, and you'll have your day in court. Bank robbery . . ."

"And murder," growled Larry.

"Hold on there!" gasped Thornley. "Just a doggone minute . . ."

"You set Parrant up," Larry calmly accused. "Burchell didn't tell us why he killed Parrant, but I'm bettin' you planned it. Burchell wasn't smart enough for . . ."

"Burchell planned it!" insisted Thornley. "We were only—waitin' for him—keepin' an eye on the street. And, when you showed up with Crazy Max, when we heard him say he'd go up to talk to Parrant . . ."

"You were afeared he'd sight your boss doin' the job," sneered Dagget, "runnin' a knife into the lawyer."

"All right—we stopped you from goin' up there," Thornley admitted. "But—hell! That ain't murder!"

"You'd have stood by and watched Max Fitch hang for it," scowled Larry.

"What did Parrant ever do to Burchell anyway?" demanded Dagget.

"He dealt himself in," sighed Thornley. "Heard Al plannin' the bank raid—and dealt himself in. Said he'd keep his mouth shut, but it'd cost us half of what we took from the vault."

Larry grinned wryly and traded stares with the deputy.

"Satisfied, Davey?"

"All right, you can quit frettin' about Fitch," muttered Dagget. "Soon as we get back to town, he'll be turned loose."

Ten minutes later and a short distance south of Coffin Canyon, they heard the echoing thud of hooves and a shouted question. The din of

225

shooting had carried far on the night-wind; Sheriff Waterbury and some of his volunteers, realizing the shots had been fired northeast of the stage route, had second thoughts about the possibility of their quarry using the old McGowan trail.

Dagget answered his chiefs challenge, identifying himself. They pressed on toward the stage trail, Dagget with the bulging sack slung from his saddle, Larry and Stretch leading the horses toting the dead and wounded. A chorus of oaths erupted from the possemen as the victorious Texans drew closer.

"Some lucky hunch Valentine had," Dagget remarked to Waterbury, as they reined up. "It was Burchell and his pards robbed the Settlers National. We tagged 'em along the McGowan road and into Coffin Canyon."

Prowse began arguing—his instinctive reaction—but the sheriff warned him to silence and cocked an attentive ear to his deputy's repetition of Thornley's statement. Nodding pensively, he declared,

"It didn't make a lick of sense anyway—Max knifin' the lawyer."

"But he might've stood trial for it," Larry pointed out.

"He might've hung for it," growled Stretch.

"Well . . ." Waterbury shrugged uncomfortably, "the sooner we get back to Logantown, the sooner Max'll be free again." The return to the county seat began, with the Texans riding level with the lawmen, and a couple of possemen taking charge of the B-Bar horses. For the first half-mile, the sheriff was taciturn and morose. "I keep thinkin' of poor Aaron," he confided. "Too bad Burchell and his men got so far from town before they were caught. By now, the westbound'll be rollin' into the depot. It'll be gone—with Mister Glynn aboard —by the time we see Main Street."

The posse was less than 200 yards from Logantown, when the county jail's only prisoner roused from slumber and spoke to the volunteer turnkey. Dan Wilson was a burly jack-of-all-trades, not the shrewdest citizen of the county, but reliable enough. Perched on a stool in the corridor, nursing a shotgun, he eyed Max curiously and a mite apprehensively.

"Need anything?" he demanded. "Water?"

"No, thanks." Max knuckled sleep from his eyes and showed the jailer a bland smile. "I think my next drink will be a beer—tall and cold. Probably around the corner at Gillery's.

Yes, Mitch Gillery serves the best draught beer in town."

"The way you talk," frowned Wilson, "it's as if you're lookin' to be turned loose in a little while." He shook his head sadly. "And you bein' held for murder."

"I *will* be released in a little while," Max assured him.

"You know somethin' I don't know?" challenged Wilson.

"Saw it all in a dream just now," shrugged Max.

"Aw, for Pete's sake . . ." began Wilson.

"It was very clear," said Max. "Sheriff Waterbury's office was crowded. He sent Deputy Dagget to bring me out and, before I left, he shook my hand." He added, calmly and firmly, "The real murderer of Sam Parrant has paid for his crime."

"How in tarnation can you know that?" argued Wilson.

"It's an impression." Max half-closed his eyes and nodded emphatically. "Quite clear—like the dream." His eyes opened wide again. He rose from the bunk and advanced to his celldoor. "What was that?"

"You've heard it before," shrugged Wilson.

"That's the night train for Idaho and the west coast—just quittin' the depot."

"It shouldn't," said Max, shaking his head worriedly. "I've warned them—at least I've *tried* to warn them. Why don't they listen? Why don't they believe? The bridge at Garvie's Gorge is in no condition—it just isn't stong enough—to take the weight of a locomotive and tender, the caboose and a couple of passenger cars."

A few minutes later, Dan Wilson turned in his shotgun, barged through the small crowd jamming Waterbury's office and made for the nearest saloon. He needed whiskey for his nerves. It was a shattering experience, listening to the prisoner predict his own release, then going out front to find the posse had returned with four prisoners, the bank's funds had been recovered and, at Sheriff Waterbury's orders, the prisoner was to be released, the real killer of Sam Parrant having been apprehended and punished. For Dan Wilson, it was a mite too much.

"Mister Wilson told me about the bank robbery," said Max, after Dagget had ushered him into the office. "It came as a complete surprise to me, I'm sorry to say."

229

"Didn't dream about no bank robbery, huh boy?" grinned the sheriff. "Well, no matter. We got all the dinero back and turned it over to Aaron. Marcus Drew's lettin' him stash it in the safe of the Grand Western till they've built a new vault for the Settlers National." He reached for Max's hand and shook it. "You're free again, young feller. And, this time, try and stay out of trouble, huh? Maybe Mayor Ashworth and the Western Union people'll drop that other charge against you. That's up to them, but I'll put in a good word for you." He stopped grinning and eyed Max anxiously. "What's up? What's ailin' you now?"

"I'm—not sure," frowned Max, raising a hand to his brow. "It's not a clear impression. It's just—what Larry calls a hunch." He turned to the Texans. "Could we go on up to the Grand Western? Something is wrong. I don't know what—but there is *something* . . ."

"The cash is safe," insisted Waterbury. "I left Leroy and a half-dozen special deputies up there. They'll stand by till Aaron has packed every last dollar into the hotel safe."

"Will you come with me?" Max begged the Texans. "I can't explain this feeling. Something terrible is about to happen . . ."

"You ought to take him straight to a doctor," opined Dagget.

"Well, we got nothin' better to do," drawled Larry, "so we might's well walk him up to the Grand Western."

Unhurriedly, the drifters escorted Max out to the street, slipped their reins and began walking their mounts toward the big hotel. Max grimaced impatiently and grasped at Larry's arm.

"Do we have to dawdle? Let's *ride* up there. Your horses aren't tired. You and I could ride double."

"All right, boy, if you're in that much of doggone hurry," shrugged Larry. He mounted lithely and bent to offer his hand. "Take hold and swing up in back of me."

Stretch straddled his pinto and heeled it to a trot to keep pace with the sorrel. All the way to the hotel, Max fumed and fretted and repeated,

"Something terrible—a tragedy . . ."

They reached the broad porch of the Grand Western and left their mounts tethered beside a handsome calico—Deputy Prowse's own horse. In the lobby, Prowse and his companions barred their way. The Texans promptly bunched their fists and, for a few tense seconds, Prowse's front teeth were in jeopardy. And then, just as Max began pleading to be allowed speak to Aaron Hinchley, the banker came barging out of the office behind the reception desk, followed by Marcus Drew, owner of the Grand Western.

Hinchley was florid with rage. Prowse and his men gaped incredulously, because the banker was brandishing a fistful of banknotes.

"A conspiracy!" he cried. "By thunder, I'll get to the bottom of this if I have to retain the entire Pinkerton agency!"

"Counterfeit," Drew grimly announced. "All those bills recovered from Burchell and his men. Worthless—all of them."

"Somebody find my cashier!" gasped Hinchley. "I want Taflin here double-quick! Maybe he can explain how all the banknotes in that vault could become counterfeit so suddenly! By thunder, I left my office only a half-hour before closing time, and I'll swear every bill in the vault was genuine. *Where's Taflin* . . . ?"

"How do you like that?" Stretch complained. "We risked our hides to find Burchell's bunch and bring the dinero back—and it ain't worth a dime."

"Burchell didn't know that," opined Larry, staring hard at the banker.

"What's that you say?" challenged Hinchley.

"Those four hard cases put up quite a fight," Larry pointed out. "We had 'em boxed in Coffin Canyon and they did their damnedest to get away with that sack. Two killed. Two wounded. Would they risk their lives for a sack full of fake dinero?"

"That sounds reasonable," offered Max.

"Who asked *you*?" challenged Hinchley and Prowse, in perfect unison.

The dreamer recoiled from them and a brief silence followed, with Hinchley still brandishing the counterfeit bills, almost apoplectic with rage, and Prowse glowering at the Texans, and Max retreating nervously to the entrance. It was then, during that brief silence, that a voice was raised in urgent warning, a faint, quavery voice, but increasing in volume. Max started convulsively and moved out to the porch, saying,

"I think—this is *it*!"

The Texans hustled out after him. The cry was repeated and, glancing to their left, they saw the lone rider approaching from the north end of town, a gray-bearded old timer in buckskin straddling a swayback mare.

233

"Mountain man," Stretch observed.

"Old Jimmy Ivers," muttered Max. "He hunts and traps—up around the Garvie's Gorge area." He crossed to the edge of the porch, staring fixedly at the old man. "Jimmy! Jimmy Ivers! What is it?"

"Keep hollerin'—but nobody hears," complained the aged trapper, as he drew closer to the hotel. "Been hollerin' ever since I hit the edge of town, and . . ."

"What's happened, old timer?" demanded Larry.

"It's the bridge," said Jimmy Ivers. "Consarn bridge never looked like *that* before —and I oughta know—on accounts I catch a look of her a couple times a week, ever' week of the year."

"The bridge across Garvie's Gorge? What about it?" gasped Max.

"Keeled over sideways, she has," declared Ivers. "She ain't fell, but she's broke away from the east rim of the gorge. I dunno how it happened. Mebbe the storm started a shift of rock and the braces and beams moved a couple feet. That'd do it, I guess. Got to go tell the sheriff now—and I'll have to warn the railroad too . . ."

234

He kicked the mare to movement again, while Max gaped at the Texans and voiced a harrowing thought.

"The westbound! It's on its way already . . . !"

"How long ago?" demanded Larry. "You know any short-cuts, any route that could get us to the gorge ahead of 'em?"

"We *have* to make it ahead of the train!" gasped Max. "If we don't . . . !"

He left the sentence unfinished, turned and dashed to the nearest horse—Prowse's—and slipped its rein. The Texans promptly untethered their mounts and swung astride and, as inevitably as the dawn and the sunset, Leroy Prowse came barging out of the hotel and saw Max riding away on the calico with Larry and Stretch in hot pursuit.

"Horse-thief!" he yelled. "Damn that Crazy Max—he stole my horse . . . !"

Before, the Texans had hesitated to give the sorrel and the pinto full rein because of the condition of the ground. Now they threw caution to the winds. Speed was suddenly more important than their own safety; there were other lives at stake.

At a hard gallop, Max led them a mile along

the stage route to a crossroads, where they swung due west. Over the thudding of hooves, he explained,

"This is the fastest route to the foothills."

"And then . . . ?" challenged Larry.

"If I can find the old trapper's track up to the bridge, we'll have a chance," said Max. But he added, with his voice shaking, "Our *only* chance."

8

FOR the second time since sundown, a posse followed Todd Waterbury and his deputies out of Logantown. Fresh horses had been obtained from every dealer and livery stable in town and, like Max and the Texans, this second posse spared no thought for the safety of men nor beasts. Jimmy Ivers had delivered his startling news. The situation was critical and could only worsen, if the westbound were not intercepted. As Waterbury put it,

"There's not much hope the engineer would see the danger—now that it's dark again. In bright moonlight, and if the whole damn shebang had collapsed, he'd have time to size up the situation and use his brakes. But—the way Jimmy tells it . . ."

"The way Jimmy tells it," finished Dagget, "there's no danger to see from up top. He was travellin' the floor of the gorge, else he mightn't have spotted the break."

"When I catch up with Fitch . . . !" began Prowse.

237

"Aw, quit your bellyachin'!" scowled Dagget. "We should've listened to Max at the start! He was right all the time!"

The surrey carrying Crane, Rose Dawes and Taflin was rounding a bend of the regular trail to Garvie's Gorge, when the westbound train reached the foothills. Crane, glancing backward, predicted,

"We'll reach the bridge close behind the train. Sounds like the westbound is right on schedule."

"Can't you hustle that team of yours?" demanded Taflin.

"We're making good time," murmured Rose. "Like Phil said, we'll see the western foothills by sunrise."

"Is the high route so much faster?" asked Taflin. "I've heard of a trail leads down to the bottom of the gorge—an alternate route."

"No place to ford down there," Crane retorted. "The railroad bridge is still the safest way to cross."

A half-mile to the north, with the eastern foothills far to their rear, the Texans and Max Fitch were urging their panting horses up a steep ascent and darting glances to the south,

238

catching brief glimpses of smoke from the loco-motive's stack.

"It's a mite late to ask," growled Stretch, as his mount scrabbled for a footing, "but couldn't we of ride straight along the railroad route?"

"Too risky—for them," panted Max. "We'd never have over-taken the train in time. There are long sections—after the foothills—where no horseman could stay level with the tracks."

"If this damn track gets any steeper . . . !" began Larry.

"We're almost to the top!" announced Max.

A few more minutes and they were on level ground again. Stretch, glancing backward, shuddered and loosed an oath. It seemed they had climbed to dizzy heights in a very short time since penetrating the foothills. The wind lashed at them, howling; they had to yell to make themselves heard.

"This way now!" cried Max, urging the calico onward.

The Texans followed him across a 60-yard wide mesa and through a stand of pines, all the time grimly conscious that the train was drawing nearer. If they had almost reached Garvie's Gorge, so had the westbound.

"How much farther?" demanded Stretch.

"When we're through the trees . . ." began Max. He paused a moment as the calico almost stumbled, then heeled the animal again and led them clear of the timberline. "There it is!"

Directly ahead was the open ground on the east edge of the gorge. They could see only the dim outline of the bridge at first, but, when they reached the railroad tracks and began a slow, wary advance, the moonlight returned, bathing the peaks in a blue-gray glow. The steel rails gleamed all the way to the lip of the gorge. And there, where the rails should have continued onto the causeway, they saw the break; a clear gap a full three yards wide.

Larry dismounted. Stretch and Max followed his example, leading their horses a short distance north of the railroad tracks and tethering them to brush. Softly and fervently, Larry cursed. Max sighed heavily, and Stretch dug out tobacco-sack and papers and said,

"Great day in the mornin'."

"I was meant to dream my dream," breathed Max. "People laughed at me and called me crazy, but I don't care any more. I can't claim the credit for warning Logantown—old Jimmy did that. And I don't care. All that matters is we got here in time to stop the westbound."

" *Just* in time," growled Larry, drawing his Colt. "And I don't mean maybe."

They moved with him as he hustled across to the tracks. Stretch emptied his leftside holster and winced to the piercing wail of the locomotive's whistle, and then they were standing on the tracks close to the edge of the long drop, facing the oncoming train and discharging their Colts to the sky. Larry triggered twice. Stretch got off three shots, and that did it.

"*Couldn't* be a hold-up," the engineer called to his partner, as he hastily applied his brake. "Hell's bells! At this hour of night—way up here at Garvie's Gorge . . . ?"

"By the great horned toad," mumbled the fireman, after thrusting his head out to stare ahead. "It's that same lamebrained sonofagun —the one they call Crazy Max."

"*Him* again?"

"But he ain't all by himself this time."

"You think I don't have eyes to see with? I spotted those other two—and their guns."

The Texans ejected their spent shells and reloaded. They were holstering their hardware when the train halted some ten yards from where they stood. Stretch yawned and grinned. Max sighed heavily and slumped against him, while Larry cupped his hands about his mouth and bellowed to the engine crew.

"This time it's the ever-lovin' *truth*—and you better believe it!"

"What the hell . . . ?" began the engineer, as he dropped from his cabin.

"Tell your passengers to stay aboard." Larry called that advice to the conductor, who had descended from the caboose and was hurrying toward him. "You and the engineer come take a look—and then you'll know we ain't foolin'."

The conductor hesitated a moment, then moved back along the tracks, calling instructions to the people watching from the windows of the two Pullman cars. Casper Glynn thrust his head out and began a challenge, but became silent when the conductor announced,

"Nothing to worry about, folks. If you'll all keep your seats, I'll check on this little emergency, and then I'll be right back to explain the situation. There's no danger, folks. No call for alarm."

When he joined the Texans and the engine crew, they were standing closer to the lip of the gorge, studying the bridge.

"See for yourself, Chris," the engineer

242

soberly invited. "Here's a sight you ain't apt to forget in a hurry."

"I'm looking," said the conductor. "I'm— looking."

"She's at a lurch, kind of," observed the fireman. "Looks like the whole thing's about ready to drop."

"What'd that trapper say?" the engineer asked Larry. "A landslide?"

"Somethin' like that," shrugged Larry. "All it takes is for just one brace to break away from the side of the gorge. Even if you made the causeway, you couldn't have rolled more than half-way across."

"Hell, no," agreed the fireman. "Bridge couldn't support the weight—not the way she's leanin'."

"Tell me the name of the trapper," begged the conductor. "Every time I meet him, I'm gonna shake his hand and buy him all the booze he can hold."

"Ivers," said Max. "Jimmy Ivers."

"How soon can we get moving?" Two of the passengers had quit the first Pullman and were moving past the locomotive, toting their baggage. The unscheduled stop had startled Bart Morrison and Webb Kilburn; they toted their bags from their left hands and eyed the Texans warily. Morrison cursed bitterly. "*You* again!"

"And the lunatic," said Kilburn, scowling at Max.

"He's no lunatic, mister," frowned the conductor. "If I was you, I'd talk friendlier to these three gents. They've saved the lives of every soul travelling on this train."

"Storm must've loosened the supports down below," the engineer told them. "Bridge has broken clear of the edge here. Only thing we can do is reverse. The engine can push us back to the Logantown depot and . . ."

"The hell with that," growled Morrison. "Isn't there any other way we can get across?"

"Not by this bridge," said the conductor.

"I don't mean the bridge!" snapped Morrison. "Isn't there another route through the mountains?"

"If you were riding, or driving some kind of rig—which you aren't . . ." The conductor turned and gestured southward. "A trail starts over there by that mound of rock and leads clear down to the floor of the gorge. Before the bridge was built, there was a fording place

244

down below. Riders and wagons used to cross all the time, but . . ."

"That'll do us," Kilburn said briskly.

There were times when the Lone Star Hellions could be taken by surprise, and this was one of those times. Stretch was half-way through rolling a smoke, and Larry was devoting all his attention to Max, wondering if he were about to be sick, when Morrison and Kilburn whisked pistols from under their jackets and levelled them.

"No heroics this time, Texas, Morrison warned Larry. "We need those horses, and we aren't about to argue."

"You railroaders—and you, crazy boy . . ." Kilburn nodded to Max and the train-crew. "Step clear. Keep your hands high and step clear of the saddlebums—and maybe you won't get hurt."

"Make it fast!" ordered Morrison.

Max straightened up, blinking uncertainly at the levelled guns, while the Texans traded thoughtful frowns.

"Don't *think* about it," scowled Kilburn. "*Do* it!" Max and the railroadmen stepped clear of the Texans and raised their hands. "That's better. And now—you heroes—unstrap the armory. I wouldn't want for you to get tempted."

"Go ahead," said Morrison. "Unbuckle those belts and let 'em drop." Quickly he swung his gun toward the conductor. "Freeze, you!"

"Stay in the car, folks!" Despite the menacing guns, the conductor was reacting automatically to the sudden appearance of more passengers; two men and a woman were about to descend from an observation platform. "There's no danger—so long as you stay inside . . . !"

He took an involuntary step forward, a move that momentarily confused Morrison and Kilburn and then Larry took advantage by staring beyond the counterfeiters and observing,

"More of 'em comin' out. It's gonna get crowded around here."

Morrison's gun was still levelled, but he was turning for a quick backward glance, and Kilburn's attention was on the conductor, when the Texans went into action. Larry drew while dropping to his knees; Stretch filled his hand from a crouched position and their Colts roared almost simultaneously. The third report was from Morrison's pistol. He fired while Larry was dropping and his bullet tore through space occupied by Larry's brawny chest a bare second before, and then he was sagging, losing his grip of the weapon, blood welling from the ugly wound in his shoulder. Kilburn—Stretch's target—was wailing like a stricken animal. His gun had fallen and he was lurching against the wide-eyed conductor, wracked with pain and staring aghast at his right fore-arm; Stretch's bullet had torn a gash from wrist-bone to elbow.

As he rose to his full height, Larry muttered commands to the railroadmen.

"Pick up their guns and tell those passengers to get aboard."

"We've seen these galoots before," Stretch remarked.

"And now I'm curious," declared Larry.

"You were born curious," grinned Stretch.

"They threatened us with guns," frowned Max. "They—wanted our horses—and . . ."

"Wanted 'em desperate, seems to me," drawled Larry. "Conductor told 'em about the down-trail to the river and, rightaway, they got the drop on us. They got someplace to go, and they're in one helluva hurry—and I wonder why."

"Everybody get aboard!" the conductor yelled.

This time, well and truly intimidated, the passengers obeyed. Morrison had become a huddled, unconscious heap, ashed-faced. Kilburn was on his knees, rocking from side to side, mumbling incoherently, until the fireman made to pick up the fallen valise. Suddenly desperate, Kilburn tried to rise.

"Don't touch that!" he gasped, his face contorting. *"Don't—touch—it . . . !"*

"What's the matter with him?" wondered Stretch. "He ashamed of his spare underwear maybe?"

"Let's find out why he's so all-fired anxious," Larry suggested. He nodded to the fireman. "Open that thing."

"No . . . !" groaned Kilburn.

The valise was opened and, for a long, shocked moment, the conductor, the engineer and fireman gaped at its contents. Stretch, frowning over their shoulders, remarked, "Every time we trade shots with some hard case —he's totin' much dinero!"

"Seems that way," agreed Larry.

"Ain't there no *poor* hard cases any more?" asked Stretch.

"I wonder if they were this rich when they *came* to Logan County," mused Larry. He tapped the conductor's shoulder. "Shut the bag. Stash it in your caboose and, when you get back to Logantown, show it to the sheriff. He'll have to figure out why they . . ."

"It couldn't be loot from the bank raid," frowned Stretch. "We already nailed the galoots pulled *that* job." He swore softly and snapped his fingers. "Wait a minute! Burchell's bunch emptied the vault, but . . . !"

"But the dinero they got away with," nodded Larry, "wasn't worth a hill of beans."

"D'you suppose . . . ?" began Stretch.

He broke off, cursing in astonishment. The whole Garvie's Gorge was bathed in bright moonlight, so the driver and passengers of the surrey were easily recognized by Max. The vehicle had approached along the wagon-route running parallel with the railroad tracks. Though startled to see the westbound train stalled here, Crane would have driven on to the edge of the gorge but for the warning yells of the conductor and engine crew.

"Haul up, mister!" bellowed the engineer. "There's been a breakaway! Bridge is about to drop!"

At last aware of the danger, Crane hastily jerked back on his reins. The surrey came to a shuddering halt and, for a long and pregnant moment, Crane, Rose Dawes and Taflin stared at the Texans and their victims. Recognizing them, Kilburn began pleading with them.

"Take me along! They shot Bart and—they know about the money . . . !"

"Shuddup, damn you!" snarled Crane.

"Jay Taflin," called Max. "Where are you going—and why?"

"None of your business," growled the cashier. "Hey, Crane, get this rig moving!"

"There's a trail leads down to the floor of the gorge—and that's our only chance," muttered Crane, as he began turning his team.

"Who's Taflin?" Larry asked Max. "Where'd we hear that name before?"

"You heard Mister Hinchley calling for him," frowned Max. "Taflin is his cashier—the only other man who knew the combination to the vault."

"Runt—are you thinkin' what I'm thinkin'?" prodded Stretch.

"I'm rememberin' Taflin and his friend got baggage in that rig," said Larry, as he retreated toward the horses.

"And you're curious again," chuckled Stretch, hustling after him.

"Wait for me," begged Max.

"Better leave this to us, boy," advised Larry. Reaching the sorrel, he darted a glance after the disappearing vehicle; Crane had driven to the rock-mound where the down-trail began. To the taller Texan, Larry opined, "We mightn't have to chase 'em all the way down. The way that hombre's racin' his team, he's liable to overturn the rig."

The Texans got mounted, wheeled their horses and made for the rock-mound, the animals' hooves clattering over the railroad tracks, raising sparks. Not as quickly, but with grim determination, Max swung astride Deputy Prowse's calico and followed.

When, a few minutes later, Sheriff Waterbury and his posse reached the gorge, the conductor and the engine-crew were still in a state of confusion; they hadn't gotten around to loading the wounded counterfeiters into the caboose, nor to closing the valise.

While Deputy Dagget examined the currency, the conductor described the violent events of the past ten minutes to Waterbury and Prowse. The bumptious deputy was in a mood to bombard the conductor with questions, but Waterbury had other ideas.

"I'm puttin' you in charge of these wounded men and the dinero," he announced. "You're travellin' back to Logantown on the train. Soon as you get there, stash these jaspers in cells and send for a doctor—also Aaron Hinchley." Ignoring Prowse's protests, he turned to the conductor. "You said Max Fitch identified one of the folks in the surrey—called him Taflin?"

"That was the name—I'm sure of it," nodded the conductor.

"It has to mean somethin'," Waterbury assured Dagget, as they remounted. "And I don't mean somethin' fair-square and honest."

"Taflin makin' a run for it," frowned Dagget.

"With Valentine and Emerson on his tail, he'll get no further than the east bank of the river," predicted the sheriff.

A short time before, the Texans and the prophet had hustled their mounts up a steep grade in their haste to reach the gorge and intercept the westbound. Now they made an even more perious journey, travelling a trail just as steep, but downhill and breakneck speed. They were descending a broken section of the gorge's east wall, at intervals glimpsing the fast-moving river far below. To their right, the edge of the trail slanted away to a sheer drop. To their left, outcroppings of brush stretched in their path, bedevilling the horses, scratching at the Texans' clothing and whisking Max's hat away.

In the rocking surrey, Rose Dawes clung to the back of the driver's seat and gasped a warning.

"You'll kill us all—if you don't slow down!"

"Watch those turns!" cried Taflin, hugging his valise to his chest, darting a horrified glance to the right. "Hell, Crane, you almost quit the trail . . ."

"They'll be after us, damnitall!" fretted Crane. He had changed in the past few minutes, and the change shocked Rose. The urbane, always serene schemer, was wild-eyed with alarm, sweating and cursing. "You saw them, didn't you? They've caught Morrison and Kilburn! It won't take Waterbury long to check on their movements, to find out they were staying at my place . . . !"

He hustled his team around the last bend and down a rutted slope, down to the floor of Garvie's Gorge, where the river ran fast, its banks littered with boulders. Staying on the

253

course of the trail, Crane made straight for the water, and the woman protested again.

"No, Phil! You *can't* . . . !"

"This is the regular fording place!" insisted Crane.

"There was a storm—have you forgotten?" challenged Taflin, leaning forward to grasp his shoulders. "The river's in flood—running too fast! We daren't try to ford here!"

A few yards from the water's edge, Crane hauled on his reins and wheeled his team sharply. The surrey swerved and skidded, almost overturning, then thudding back onto all four wheels. He discarded his whip and climbed down.

"I'll take a closer look" he decided. "It mightn't be as deep as it appears."

"It's too deep for horses or a rig," argued Taflin.

He dropped from the surrey, clinging to his valise and neglecting to offer a hand to Rose, who grimaced in disgust and climbed down.

"Don't get so excited you'd drop that," she warned, gesturing to the valise. "Remember half of it is mine."

About to move across to the bank to stand beside Crane, she paused, staring toward the slope. Her scalp crawled as the thud of hooves reached her ears. Crane heard it too and, with a violent oath, dashed past her to return to the surrey.

"If you're carrying a gun, use it!" he yelled to Taflin.

Apprehensive, but dangerous, the cashier drew a pocket-pistol from inside his coat. And then, just as Crane reached the surrey, Max and the Texans appeared, pounding down the slant and calling a challenge. Taflin opened fire and his shooting was fast and inaccurate—all but one wild slug. Larry heard Max's startled cry, as he brought his sorrel to a slithering halt and dropped to the ground. The calico reared, nickering, and Max fell heavily, blood staining his jacket at the left side. Stretch, still mounted, loosed an oath, drew his righthand gun and cut loose in angry retaliation. From a half-prone position. Larry joined in.

Crouched by the surrey, Crane drew a pistol and got off his first shot. The bullet struck soggy ground inches from the face of the fallen dreamer, spattering mud and grit into his eyes and temporarily blinding him. In panic, Max rose to all fours and tried crawling.

"The rocks!" Larry called to Stretch. "You make for the rocks. I'll take care of Max."

"Move then," urged Stretch. "I'll give you cover."

He triggered again and, with a choking gasp, Taflin relled and collapsed. Another slug from the taller Texan's Colt seared the rump of a team-horse with the inevitable result. The animal bounded forward and the other teamer kept pace. About to climb aboard, Crane only had time to grasp the handle of his valise before the surrey rolled past, leaving him exposed to Stretch's fire.

But Stretch had ceased fire long enough to hustle his and the other two horses toward the clump of boulders some fifteen yards to his right, following Larry, who had picked Max up and draped him across his shoulders.

Crane's next action took Rose Dawes by surprise. The saloonkeeper stared after the surrey. It was still in sight, but he could not hope to reach it before the Texans got into position. From the safe cover of those rocks, he would be a clear target. But they still hadn't reached the rocks, and he took full advantage of the lapse in the shooting.

Taflin lay on his back, groaning, clutching

256

his valise. Dropping to one knee beside him, Crane snatched the valise from him opened his own and emptied Taflin's share of the loot into it. Taflin gasped a protest, but lacked the strength to forestall him. Chuckling harshly, he leapt to his feet and hurried across to where Rose stood.

"I guess you've heard the old expresssion," he grinned. "Every man for himself."

"What are you—doing . . . ?" she gasped, as he moved around behind her.

She struggled wildley, as his left arm crooked about her neck. The valise, its handle gripped tight in his left hand, blocked her view of the rocks behind which the Texans had taken cover. The pistol, steady in Crane's right hand, was cocked and aimed at the rocks.

"You aren't much help in a showdown," he muttered to the woman, "so I just have to use you the best way I can."

"*Use* me . . . ?"

"You're my shield, sweetheart. They won't shoot for fear of hitting you. I'll order them to come out with their hands up—and they'll have to obey."

"Phil—we made a bargain . . . !"

"All deals are off," Crane said bluntly. "He

travels faster who travels alone. As soon as I'm rid of those heroes, I'll go find the surrey and be on my way. Or maybe I'll take one of their horses."

"You have to take me with you! You *promised* . . . !"

Ignoring her tears, her screamed accusations, he yelled to the Texans.

"If you fire, the woman dies! Show yourselves—I mean *now*! Come out of there with your hands up!"

Sprawled beside Larry and Max, Stretch raised himself on an elbow and scanned the area between the rocks and the river. He could see Crane near the water's edge, grasping a valise and something considerably more valuable, a good-looking woman who struggled to free herself.

"He ain't foolin'," he warned Larry. "Got himself a shield-human and female and purty."

"Sonofabitch," scowled Larry.

"That's Rose Dawes from the Wheel Of Fortune," offered Max. He clasped a hand to his side, winced and mumbled a desperate lie. "I'm not—in great pain. It's only a scratch . . ."

"You got a deep crease there, boy," growled

258

Larry. "Wouldn't surprise me if the bullet dented a rib."

"Well—we have to go out anyway," said Max. "He has a hostage—and that gives him the advantage."

"I won't wait!" roared Crane.

"I'll go first," Larry said quietly. "Listen now—I'll only have to time to say this the once. If I show myself and get close enough, I might get to score on him without hittin' the woman." As he began rising, he muttered a last command to his partner. "Your second Colt—stick it in the back of my belt."

Stretch unsheathed his leftside Colt, nudged it into the back of Larry's pants and rose with him.

"Keep coming!" barked Crane. "And get rid of those guns!"

Larry, moving slightly ahead of Stretch so as to block Crane's view of his second holster, tossed his Colt away to the left. Stretch emptied his rightside holster and did likewise. They advanced to within twelve feet of Crane and the woman, then halted to his command.

"That's far enough!" He bared his teeth in a grin of triumph. "Had to interfere, didn't you? Well—by Judas—it's gonna cost you!"

"Phil . . . !" gasped the woman.

"I said *raise those hands!*" snarled Crane.

Stretch began raising his hands. Larry was lifting his left, his right still hanging free, his eyes searching for an exposed section of Crane's anatomy, when the unexpected happened. Rose had struggled in vain. She had used her elbows to jab at Crane, but to no effect. In this last moment of crisis, with the crook of Crane's arm against her mouth, her left hand was still free, and she used it. The nails dug into the back of the hand grasping the valise. She clawed with all her might, and Crane loosed a wail of pain. He still clung to her, but lost his grip of the valise.

As the bag dropped, Larry whisked the Colt from his pants-belt, hammered back and fired, and the well-aimed slug missed Rose by an inch and seared Crane's ribs. Crane cursed bitterly and, feeling his grip weaken, the woman pulled free of his grasp and dropped to her knees. At deadly short range Crane's pistol barked at Larry, but he was throwing himself sideways, anticipating the saloonkeeper's action. His Colt roared and, this time, he did more than burn Crane with his bullet. It slammed into Crane's chest, and the impact drove him backward. At the water's edge, he overbalanced and fell, hitting the surface of the fast-running stream with a splash. When he reappeared, he was already twenty yards downstream, being carried along by the force of the current. The Texans caught a fleeting glimpse of a raised boot, and then he was gone. Weeks from now, maybe months, the body of Phil Crane would be found many miles downriver—or might never be found.

"Damn all men." That was all Rose Dawes could say. She squatted beside the valise, her head bowed, her shoulders heaving. "He wasn't any different from all the others. They promise —and then they double-cross—they let you down. Damn them. Damn all men . . ."

"Take a look in the bag," urged Larry, as he returned Stretch's gun.

Stretch unfastened the catches of the valise, raised the lid and stared at the green bundles.

"Mucho dinero," he grunted. "Every time we have us a shoot-out with some hard case— we find out he's loaded—rich as a king."

"You said that before," muttered Larry. He retrieved his and Stretch's Colts and eyed the woman expectantly. "Anything you want to tell us?"

261

"Go to hell," sighed Rose Dawes.

Larry ambled across to kneel beside Taflin, who was staring up at the moonlit sky, a hand clasped to his bloodied chest. He groaned a protest, as Larry nudged the hand away and began a cursory examination. Stretch joined them and scratched a match or two, the better to permit his partner to inspect the wound. Taflin still bled, but the wound was superfluous; the bullet had not lodged. Three inches of skin below the left breast had been gashed, a shallow graze from which Taflin would soon recover.

"Looks bad," observed Stretch, after trading winks with his partner.

"About as bad as it could get," muttered Larry.

"I was a damn fool," groaned Taflin. "I let my hate get the better of me—and cloud my judgement. I hated Aaron Hinchley—and wanted Rose—but now I realize she was only —only using me . . ."

"Listen feller, I don't know how long you'll last," said Larry.

"If you hanker to talk—talk fast," advised Stretch, "while you're strong enough for it."

Taflin was still conscious, still talking and

considerably healthier than he realized, when Waterbury, Dagget and their volunteers reached the scene. Max had bathed his face, swabbing the mud and grit from his eyes by lying prone at the water's edge with Stretch to steady him. Rose Dawes still squatted on the damp ground, heedless of the damage to her travelling gown. Over and over again, she mumbled,

"Damn all men."

"Max got creased and so did the cashier jasper," Stretch informed the sheriff. "You'll find a fat passel of greenbacks in that valise, which used to belong to a feller named Crane. You can ask my partner all about it. He's gettin' the whole story from Taflin."

Very carefully, his lined face as calm as if he were handling such large sums every day of the week, Waterbury checked the contents of the valise. "Better than sixty thousand," he told Dagget. "I'm no expert, but I'd say it's the genuine article."

"As genuine as what them other hombres were totin'," frowned Dagget.

"There names are Morrison and Kilburn," said Larry. "Seems they set up the whole deal with the saloonkeeper—Crane. A switch, Sheriff. A swap."

"Some swap," commented Dagget. "Some helluva swap."

"Morrison and Kilburn supplied the fake greenbacks," said Larry. "Taflin worked the swap—in the vault of the Settlers National. I'll explain it to you, while we're travellin' back to Logantown."

"Howdy, Rose," drawled Dagget. "You mixed into this mess?"

"Damn all men," said Rose.

"That looks like Phil Crane's rig," said Dagget, staring along the bank to where the surrey-team had finished their hectic run. "Is Crane here too?"

"Where *is* Crane?" demanded Taflin, vaguely surprised that he could still talk and move. Haggard and trembling, he struggled to a sitting posture. "He got me into this! Crane and that double-crossing whore! She never did want me! She was Crane's woman . . . !"

"Crane's dead," Larry flatly informed the lawmen. He jerked a thumb toward the river. "Went like a real hero. Used the woman for a shield."

"I figure he'd have gunned us down, if the

woman hadn't clawed him," frowned Stretch. "Wasn't for her, you couldn't of got a shot at him."

"Well . . ." Waterbury nodded grimly, "that's *somethin'* in her favour."

Stretch retrieved the surrey and team, while Larry helped Max astride the calico. They put Taflin and the woman on the back seat of the surrey, and Dagget elected to drive. And then, while the Texans were remounting and the surrey and its escort were starting up the slant, Max half-closed his eyes and raised a hand to his temple.

"Look out," grinned Stretch. "He's about to see another consarn vision."

"How about it, Max?" asked Larry, taking the calico's rein. "What d'you see?"

"I'm not in great pain," mumbled Max. "I won't faint—till we get back to town. She'll weep over me." He grinned sheepishly. "Hard to believe, huh? Well, it's going to happen. Louise—beautiful Louise—will weep over me."

"Damn near worth gettin' creased by a bullet," opined Stretch.

By mid-morning Saturday, Logantown folk

were unanimous on the subject of Max Fitch, his character, his aspirations, his strange powers, and the general attitude was expressed by Doc Milford, who declared,

"Folks'll be sceptical. Folks'll always be sceptical, I guess. But they won't laugh at him any more, and they won't call him crazy. He was right about the bridge. Couldn't tell us *when* it'd fall, but at least he tried to warn us."

On the porch of the law office, Sheriff Waterbury puffed contentedly at a cigar and traded a few last words with Larry and Stretch. Their horses awaited them at the hitch-rail, saddlebags bulging, packrolls lashed into position; they were about to take their leave of Logantown.

"What scares me," the boss-lawman confided, "is the thought that Crane and his crooked friends might've gotten away with it, but for Burchell decidin' to rob the Settlers National last night. Some coincidence, huh?"

"Burchell and Taflin both had the same idea," Larry reminded him. "They wanted to hurt the banker by hittin' his bank while his boss was in town."

"I guess you've heard by now," offered Waterbury. "Mister Glynn travelled south to

Somerville this morning with the westbound passengers. He'll connect with a Burton and Keene stage at Somerville and ride it to the railhead at Moransburg. Won't be any train crossin' Garvie's Gorge for many a long week. Railroad engineers got quite a chore ahead of 'em, settin' the bridge to rights."

Deputy Dagget emerged from the office and raised a hand in nonchalant salute, as the Texans descended to the hitch-rail.

"Stop by again," he invited.

"Well, that ain't likely," drawled Stretch. "We scarce ever come back. We just keep movin' on, you know?"

"Prisoners givin' you trouble?" asked Larry.

"*That'll* be the day," grinned Dagget. "they've been doctored and now they're cussin' one another—Morrison and Kilburn cussin' Taflin—Thornley and Cardew cussin' Morrison and Kilburn. One big happy family—I don't think."

After being farewelled by the lawmen, the Texans rode north along Main and reined up by the ground floor gallery of the Grand Western, where a smiling Max Fitch socialized with Louise Hinchley, her father and Doc Milford.

267

"You said goodbye to Pike?" asked Max.

"When we collected our horses," nodded Larry. "You okay now, boy?"

"He wasn't scratched up bad," drawled Doc. "Be good as new in a couple of days."

"This community is indebted to my young friend Max," Hinchley warmly declared, "and to you gentlemen from Texas."

"Mister Glynn was very impressed," smiled Louise.

"Impressed?" frowned Stretch. "You mean by the looks of the Settlers National? Heck, ma'am, it looks plumb toilworn."

"I mean he was impressed by the quick recovery of all the stolen money," said Louise.

"Oh, sure," shrugged Stretch. "Well, a banker'd be bound to appreciate a thing like *that*."

"The bank's funds recovered in a matter of hours," enthused Hinchley. "By Godfrey, you should have seen the expression on old Cass Glynn's face when the train came back to Logantown. He was grateful to be alive. And then—when he learned the cash had been recovered and the thieves apprehended . . ."

"Like Miss Louise said," drawled Doc, "the big man was impressed."

"Larry, I thought you'd like to know," said Max, "Mister Hinchley has consented to my calling on Louise—as often as I wish."

"I'm old, but not stubborn," Hinchley cheerfully assured the Texans. "Prove I'm wrong, and I'll admit it and try to make amends. I saw Max as a muddle-headed dreamer, but now I'm glad to acknowledge his true worth. His predictions aren't always accurate, but . . ."

"But he was right about the bridge at Garvie's Gorge," said Larry.

"He was right," nodded the banker. "And we'll never forget it."

"Larry—Stretch—thanks for everything," said Max, as the Texans raised their hands in farewell.

"Our pleasure," shrugged Larry. "Take care, boy."

"Hold on just a second there," muttered Doc. He descended from the porch, produced an unlabelled bottle from under his coat and jammed it into Larry's saddlebag. "A little comfort for the trail—you know what I mean?"

"Sure appreciate that, Doc," grinned Larry.

"If we spike our coffee with that stuff," warned Stretch, "the beans are gonna leap clear outa the pot."

Unhurriedly, the Texans ambled their mounts toward Logantown's outskirts. Max, Doc, Louise and the banker stared after them, watching until they were lost from sight at a turn of the main stem. And then, raising a hand to his brow, half-closing his eyes, Max muttered a prediction.

"There'll be no peace for Larry and Stretch. Wherever they roam, they'll find upheaval and danger and strife."

Doc Milford chuckled softly, lit a cigar and remarked,

"Boy, you didn't need to be a prophet to know *that*. There'll never be a quiet time for the Texas Hell-Raisers."

THE END

FARGO: PANAMA GOLD
by John Benteen

Cleve Buckner was recruiting an army of killers, gunmen and deserters from all over Central America. With foreign money behind him, Buckner was going to destroy the Panama Canal before it could be completed. Fargo's job was to stop Buckner—and to eliminate him once and for all!

FARGO: THE SHARPSHOOTERS
by John Benteen

The Canfield clan, thirty strong, were raising hell in Texas. One of them had shot a Texas Ranger, and the Rangers had to bring in the killer. Fargo was tough enough to hold his own against the whole clan.

SUNDANCE: OVERKILL
by John Benteen

Sundance's reputation as a fighting man had spread. There was no job too tough for the halfbreed to handle. So when a wealthy banker's daughter was kidnapped by the Cheyenne, he offered Sundance $10,000 to rescue the girl.

HELL RIDERS
by Steve Mensing

Wade Walker's kid brother, Duane, was locked up in the Silver City jail facing a rope at dawn. Wade was a ruthless outlaw, but he was smart, and he had vowed to have his brother out of jail before morning!

DESERT OF THE DAMNED
by Nelson Nye

The law was after him for the murder of a marshal—a murder he didn't commit. Breen was after him for revenge—and Breen wouldn't stop at anything . . . blackmail, a frameup . . . or murder.

DAY OF THE COMANCHEROS
by Steven C. Lawrence

Their very name struck terror into men's hearts—the Comancheros, a savage army of cutthroats who swept across Texas, leaving behind a bloodstained trail of robbery and murder.

SUNDANCE: SILENT ENEMY
by John Benteen

Both the Indians and the U.S. Cavalry were being victimized. A lone crazed Cheyenne was on a personal war path against both sides. They needed to pit one man against one crazed Indian. That man was Sundance.

LASSITER
by Jack Slade

Lassiter wasn't the kind of man to listen to reason. Cross him once and he'd hold a grudge for years to come—if he let you live that long. But he was no crueler than the men he had killed, and he had never killed a man who didn't need killing.

LAST STAGE TO GOMORRAH
by Barry Cord

Jeff Carter, tough ex-riverboat gambler, now had himself a horse ranch that kept him free from gunfights and card games. Until Sturvesant of Wells Fargo showed up. Jeff owed him a favour and Sturvesant wanted it paid up. All he had to do was to go to Gomorrah and recover a quarter of a million dollars stolen from a stagecoach!

McALLISTER ON THE COMANCHE CROSSING
by Matt Chisholm

The Comanche, deadly warriors and the finest horsemen in the world, reckon McAllister owes them a life—and the trail is soaked with the blood of the men who had tried to outrun them before.

QUICK-TRIGGER COUNTRY
by Clem Colt

Turkey Red hooked up with Curly Bill Graham's outlaw crew and soon made a name for himself. But wholesale murder was out of Turk's line, so when range war flared he bucked the whole border gang alone . . .

PISTOL LAW
by Paul Evan Lehman

Lance Jones came back to Mustang for just one thing—Revenge! Revenge on the people who had him thrown in jail; on the crooked marshal; on the human vulture who had already taken over the town. Now it was Lance's turn . . .

GUNSLINGER'S RANGE
by Jackson Cole

Three escaped convicts are out for revenge. They won't rest until they put a bullet through the head of the dirty snake who locked them behind bars.

RUSTLER'S TRAIL
by Lee Floren

Jim Carlin knew he would have to stand up and fight because he had staked his claim right in the middle of Big Ike Outland's best grass. Jim also had a score to settle with his renegade brother.

Larry and Stretch:
THE TRUTH ABOUT SNAKE RIDGE
by Marshall Grover

The troubleshooters came to San Cristobal to help the needy. For Larry and Stretch the turmoil began with a brawl, then an ambush, and then another attempt on their lives—all in one day.

WOLF DOG RANGE
by Lee Floren

Montana was big country, but not big enough for a ruthless land-grabber like Will Ardery. He would stop at nothing, unless something stopped him first—like a bullet from Pete Manly's gun.

Larry and Stretch: DEVIL'S DINERO
by Marshall Grover

Plagued by remorse, a rich old reprobate hired the Texas Troubleshooters to deliver a fortune in greenbacks to each of his victims. Even before Larry and Stretch rode out of Cheyenne, a traitor was selling the secret and the hunt was on.

CAMPAIGNING
by Jim Miller

Ambushed on the Santa Fe trail, Sean Callahan is saved from dying by two Indian strangers. Then the trio is joined by a former slave called Hannibal. But there'll be more lead and arrows flying before the band join the legendary Kit Carson in his campaign against the Comanches.

DONOVAN
by Elmer Kelton

Donovan was supposed to be dead. The town had buried him years before when Uncle Joe Vickers had fired off both barrels of a shotgun into the vicious outlaw's face as he was escaping from jail. Now Uncle Joe had been shot—in just the same way.

CODE OF THE GUN
by Gordon D. Shirreffs

MacLean came riding home with saddle-tramp written all over him, but sewn in his shirt-lining was an Arizona Ranger's star. MacLean had his own personal score to settle—in blood and violence!

GAMBLER'S GUN LUCK
by Brett Austen

Gamblers hands are clean and quick with cards, guns and women. But their names are black, and they seldom live long. Parker was a hell of a gambler. It was his life—or his death . . .

ORPHAN'S PREFERRED
by Jim Miller

A boy in a hurry to be a man, Sean Callahan answers the call of the Pony Express. With a little help from his Uncle Jim and the Navy Colt .36, Sean fights Indians and outlaws to get the mail through.

DAY OF THE BUZZARD
by T. V. Olsen

All Val Penmark cared about was getting the men who killed his wife. All young Jason Drum cared about was getting back his family's life savings. He could not understand the ruthless kind of hate Penmark nursed in his guts.

THE MANHUNTER
by Gordon D. Shirreffs

Lee Kershaw knew that every Rurale in the territory was on the lookout for him. But the offer of $5,000 in gold to find five small pieces of leather was too good to turn down.

RIFLES ON THE RANGE
by Lee Floren

Doc Mike and the farmer stood there alone between Smith and Watson. Doc Mike knew what was coming. There was this moment of stillness, a clock-tick of eternity, and then the roar would start. And somebody would die . . .

HARTIGAN
by Marshall Grover

Hartigan had come to Cornerstone to die. He chose the time and the place, but he did not fight alone. Side by side with Nevada Jim, the territory's unofficial protector, they challenged the killers—and Main Street became a battlefield.

HARSH RECKONING
by Phil Ketchum

The minute Brand showed up at his ranch after being illegally jailed, people started shooting at him. But five years of keeping himself alive in a brutal prison had made him tough and careless about who he gunned down . . .

RENEGADE'S TRAIL
by Gordon D. Shirreffs

No man except Lee Kershaw was strong enough or clever enough to track down the infamous half-breed Queho. But he had been Queho's friend. Lee knew he would have to kill him to succeed—or be killed . . .

FARGO: MASSACRE RIVER
by John Benteen

Fargo spurred his horse to the edge of the road. The ambushers up ahead had now blocked the road. Fargo's convoy was a jumble, a perfect target for the insurgents' weapons!

SUNDANCE:
DEATH IN THE LAVA
by John Benteen

The land echoed with the thundering hoofs of Modoc ponies. In minutes they swooped down and captured the wagon train and its cargo of gold. But now the halfbreed they called Sundance was going after it, and he swore nothing would stand in his way.

GUNS OF FURY
by Ernest Haycox

Dane Starr, alias Dan Smith, wanted to close the door on his past and hang up his guns, but people wouldn't let him. Good men wanted him to settle their scores for them. Bad men thought they were faster and itched to prove it. Starr had to keep killing just to stay alive.